S0-ARL-272

Peregrine

Peregrine

Joan Elizabeth Goodman

Houghton Mifflin Company

The text of this book is set in 12-point Janson Text.
Map by Joan Elizabeth Goodman

Library of Congress Cataloging-in-Publication Data

Goodman, Joan E.
Peregrine / Joan Elizabeth Goodman.
p. cm.
Sequel to: The winter hare.
Summary: In 1144, fifteen-year-old Lady Edith, having lost her husband and child and anxious to avoid marrying a man she detests, sets out from her home in Surrey to go on a pilgrimage to Jerusalem.
ISBN 0-395-97729-0
[1. Pilgrims and pilgrimages Fiction. 2. Self-perception Fiction. 3. Middle Ages Fiction.] I. Title.
PZ7.G61375Pg 2000
[Fic] — dc21
99-19041
CIP

Manufactured in the United States of America
QUM 10 9 8 7 6 5 4 3 2

For Keith, my fellow pilgrim.

Contents

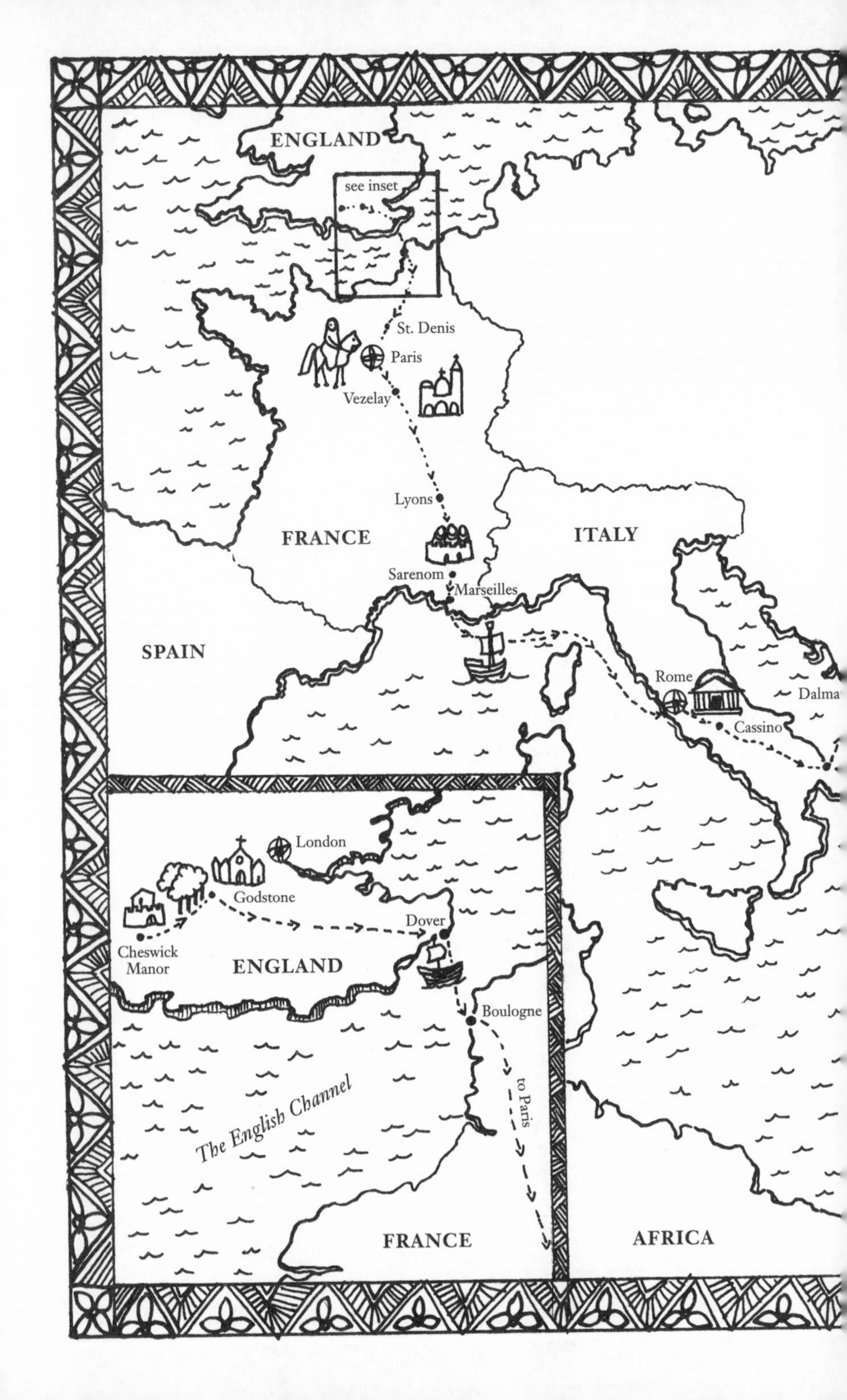
ENGLAND
see inset
St. Denis
Paris
Vezelay
Lyons
FRANCE
ITALY
Sarenom
Marseilles
SPAIN
Rome
Dalma
Cassino
London
Godstone
Dover
Cheswick
Manor
ENGLAND
Boulogne
to Paris
The English Channel
FRANCE
AFRICA

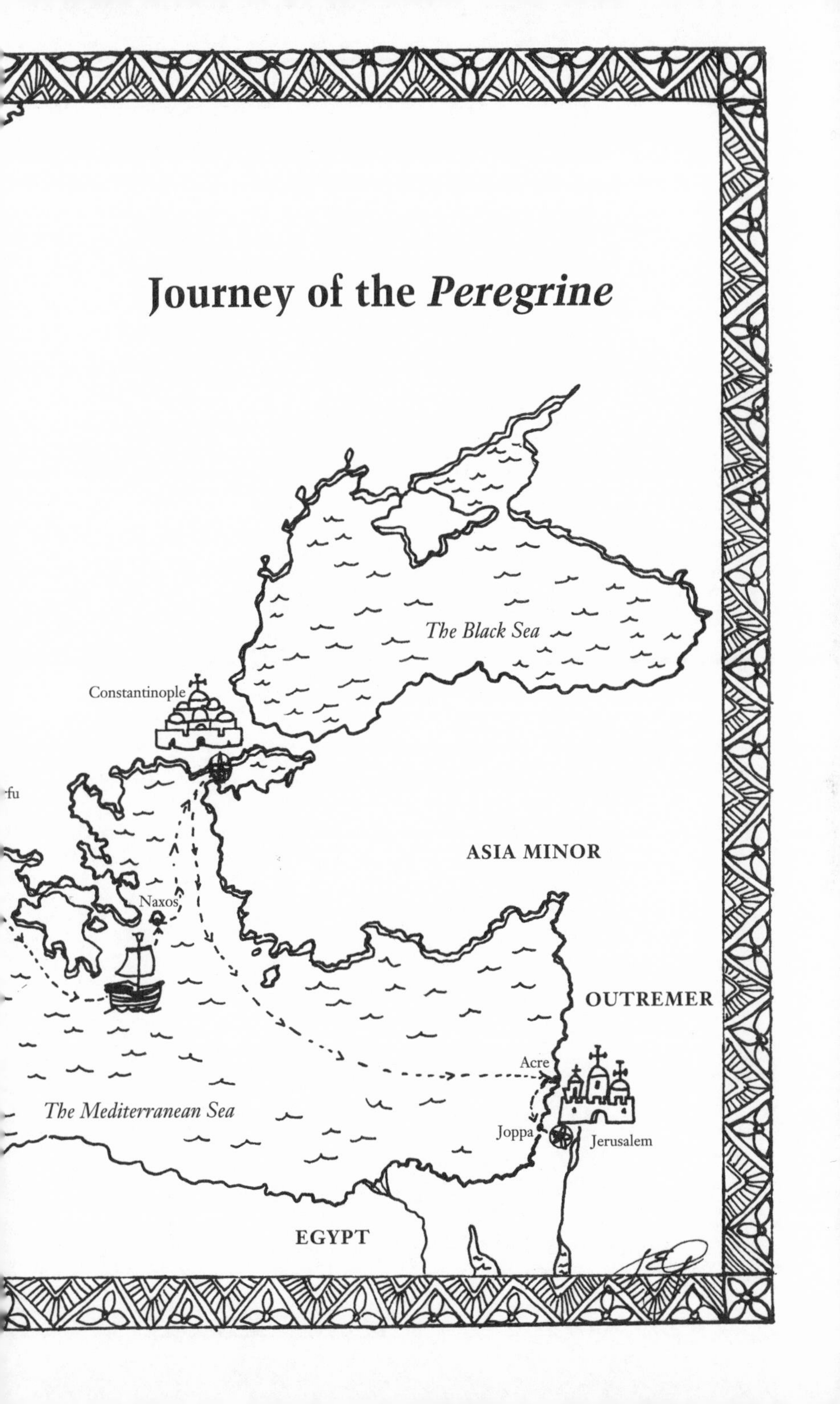
Journey of the *Peregrine*
The Black Sea
Constantinople
ASIA MINOR
Naxos
OUTREMER
Acre
The Mediterranean Sea
Joppa
Jerusalem
EGYPT

Peregrine

I.
Ambush

"Lady Edith, do you not bid farewell to your husband and child?" asked Dame Joan, reining in her palfrey at the top of the little knoll that looked down on Cheswick.

"Nay."

"I should think you'd take a moment to look back," the old nettle persisted.

"You may stop as you please," I said, spurring my little mare to a swift canter. She could gaze forever at Cheswick Manor if she wished. I would not say good-bye. I'd not look back at the graves of Sir Bohemund, my husband, and my little babe. I hadn't wanted to go on living without them, but my life persisted whether I willed it or not.

"You must weep," Dame Joan had insisted, in the weeks following their deaths.

But I wouldn't. Once I started weeping, there'd be no end of tears. Besides, my grief was my own. I didn't wish to show it, or share it with the world. I closed the door of my sorrow, and locked it. No matter what Dame Joan said. That is how it would be.

April second, in the year of our Lord, 1144, I was fifteen years old and able to do what I wanted for the first time in my life. Naturally, my parents had suggestions, but a widow of means could make some of her own decisions. Sir Bohemund had left me my dower and a generous marriage portion. I would use part of it to leave my home in Surrey. I could have stayed on, a chamber in the guest house would have been set aside for Dame Joan and me, but I could no longer abide the stones of Cheswick. It certainly pleased my stepson and his new wife to have me gone. Perhaps someday I might return to a small holding near Godalming. I couldn't look that far ahead, now.

I had my father's reluctant blessing, the wholehearted approval of the Church, and I was going to the Outremer, beyond the sea, to the Holy Land. I'd go to Jerusalem, the navel of the world — the Omphalus. The thought made my skin itch and my blood rush as nothing else had these past months. I didn't care about the shrines and holy relics, although I let Dame Joan believe that this was a pilgrimage dedicated to His glory and my own salvation. I wanted to see what lay outside the small world I'd known. But, most of all, I was afraid.

Since my husband's death, Sir Runcival of Surrey

had come twice to Cheswick Manor. He was an odious man who claimed friendship with Sir Bohemund. But my good lord had had nothing to do with the grasping Sir Runcival. Now I feared he was plotting to wed me. I didn't want to be married off again, especially not to Sir Runcival. Yet, if I remained in England, King Stephen could force me to marry. So I chose pilgrimage. I didn't care how difficult and dangerous it might be.

There was something else, as well, something I could not name. It was as if I were suffocating in England. Once my homeland was behind me, and Jerusalem ahead of me, I was sure I'd be able to breathe freely.

We were going first to Godstone Abbey, where served my brother Simon. He, and several other friars, were traveling to Pope Lucius II in Rome. It was very convenient for me to go with them and their guard. From Rome I would journey on with one of the pilgrim groups to Jerusalem.

I soon came abreast of Sir Howard, my seneschal. My *former* seneschal. Once he'd delivered me to Godstone Abbey, he'd return to Cheswick in service of my stepson.

"Milady, do not tire your mount ere the journey's begun," said Sir Howard. "It's a long ride to Godstone Abbey."

I might have been "milady," but someone was always telling me what to do. I reined in my mare and continued at a stately and boring pace. I didn't want to punish my little mare; I only wanted to be free.

Patience, I thought. Although it had been nearly impossible, I *had* learned patience. At least, I'd learned to appear patient, first at Woburn Abbey where I was sent the year before my marriage. Sir Bohemund was as kind to me as my own father, but he could not marry a wild girl. I had to learn to be a proper mistress for Cheswick Manor. Patience, the nuns reminded me constantly, was essential. I was sick of patience, and missed my impatient self. Perhaps when I got to Godstone and saw my brother Simon, he'd help me find again the girl I'd been. I would try to be patient until then.

"Lady Edith," said Dame Joan. "Put your hood up; you'll take a chill."

I didn't feel the cold, but it was simpler not to argue. So I pulled the fur-lined hood over my wimple.

"That's better," she said, adjusting her own cloak.

Dame Joan looked cold, poor old red-nosed thing. It was wrong to drag her away from the warmth of hearth and home. But she'd not let me go without her, and I *had* to go. At least I made sure that her traveling cloak was as fine and warm as my own.

We were soon past the village and fields that I knew. Most of my married life I'd been shut up indoors with the endless tasks of spinning and stitching under the watchful eye of Dame Joan. No rambles in the woods for me. There was that one time I'd run away, yet that was different.

When I was with child, I was even more confined. But then I had something to care about, and I didn't mind so much.

Once past the town of Woking, where I'd been to three fairs, all was new and strange to me. I liked the newness, and even more, the strangeness. Now, I minded not the slow pace. It gave me time to think about the villages and manors we passed, and the people who lived in them. How different would my life have been if I lived by that stream, or on yonder hilltop? I rode on, wondering.

"Milady!" called Peter, my page.

I stopped, and Peter caught up with me. I'd gotten so lost in my thoughts, I'd gone far beyond my train.

"We must ride into the king's forest," said Peter, "and Sir Howard bids us stay close together. You are supposed to be in the middle of the line with Dame Joan."

"Very well," I said and smiled at Peter. Even this little imp told me what to do.

I turned back and took my place beside Dame Joan.

"I should think you'd pay a little heed, Lady Edith. Going off alone, and near the king's forest."

I'd nearly forgotten that the road went through the forest.

"Sir Howard says we must go quickly and be ready to flee if he gives the alarm."

"Yes, yes," I said.

Perhaps I should have been afraid of the forest. England was still savaged by the war between Empress Matilda and the usurper, King Stephen, for the throne. Many barons used the chaos of war for their own evil ends. The bands of the Earl of Essex often waylaid the innocent under the pretext of serving the king. What better place for knaves to lurk than in the gloom of the forest? I shuddered. I would not want to fall into Essex's hands. But the forest was also a grand place — a magic place — I'd not let fear of Essex, or anyone else, spoil it.

As we rode into the vert all grew silent, lost in the greater silence of the wood. There was the occasional chirp of bird, or squirrel chatter, but the wood bred a deep hush. I could feel us all caught in its spell. As yet there were no leaves on the branches; I wished I could see it completely submerged in green. Now, only the ancient dark firs blocked out portions of the sky. The deeper we went into the forest, the colder it became. I shivered, more from excitement than the cold. Darker, colder, and more still; it was wonderful.

The forest had the thick smell of rot and decay; threaded through that was a thin, fresh scent of life beginning. It echoed the way I felt. So much of me had died with my husband and child; yet that which lived seemed determined to grow.

All around us I felt the forest creatures watching our progress. They kept vigil behind the safe curtain of thicket. Every now and then, I'd see the bright flicker of an eye, or the rustling that betrayed a living presence. Did they wonder about me as I did them? Were they as tensed and ready to fight or flee as the men around me, who now proceeded with swords drawn? I fancied how it would be to give up everything I'd ever known of life to bury myself in this untamed, wonderful place. It wouldn't take much to shelter and feed myself. With some practice I could probably do as well as any huntsman. Of course the penalty for poaching in the king's forest was hanging. Perhaps I was better off following my own road; the forest was not for me.

Sir Howard raised his hand, and we came to an abrupt and silent halt. He'd heard something or seen something.

One of the men near me murmured "Ambush!" As still as I was, my heart began to race. Was my life ending in this wood? I stroked my mare; mayhap in soothing her, I'd calm myself. I looked all about me to see what Sir Howard had noted. Dame Joan's face was as white as her wimple. Her lips moved in silent prayer.

Then, crashing, storming its way out of the brush, nearly opposite me, it was upon us! This wild thing, slight as a hind, ran crouched over on two legs. It deftly raced through the men on horseback, eluded the lunging yeomen, and made its way straight to me.

It flung itself upon my skirts with a piercing wail. The men hastened to my aid, their swords ready to run the creature through.

"Stop!" I called, my voice faltering, for I was sore afraid. But this creature was a supplicant, not an attacker. The men held back, their weapons poised to kill.

The creature clung to my cloak, my gown, my boots — whatever it could grasp. How had it known to come to me? From my mount, all I could make of it was a mass of hair, matted and tangled with leaves and twigs. Yet soon I realized that the thin brown claws, pulling at me, were human hands. And the incoherent cries were a child's. They were so strange, yet so familiar. Finally a voice emerged.

"Help me!" it sobbed.

A face, caked with dirt, furrowed by tears, looked up at me. In that wretched face were two limpid, blue-sky eyes.

"Please, help."

It was a girl. And I saw, in those blue eyes, that I needed her.

"Yes," I said. "Yes, I'll help."

II.
Rhiannon

Rhiannon. Her name was Rhiannon. A Welsh name, as full of mystery and clarity as the girl herself.

"It's madness," said Dame Joan.

Not that I'd admit it, but she was right. It was madness to want to adopt this strange girl. I'm not sure what possessed me. I couldn't put it into words, certainly not to convince Dame Joan or Sir Howard. I simply knew I had to rescue her, for her sake and mine. I'd take her from the forest and care for her. Unless the girl objected, I'd take her with me to the Holy Land.

"Milady," said Sir Howard. "Dame Joan speaks true. It doesn't seem quite . . . She's got a Welsh name and the Welsh look. The Welsh, you know, they're sorcerers and witches. They're not to be trusted."

I'd heard all those stories about Welsh witches, and never paid them any heed. Why should I now?

Dame Joan crossed herself. "Just *look* at her!"

"The dirt will wash away," I said.

"And then what?"

"Then she'll be clean." I tried very hard not to smile. I knew there would be objections to keeping Rhiannon with us, but I was surprised by the vehemence of their reaction. Even Peter looked daggers at the girl. It was as if we viewed two separate beings. Where I saw a child, Dame Joan, Sir Howard, and the others saw a malignant sprite.

"Are we not holy pilgrims?" I asked.

There was grumbling in reply.

"God has favored us with an opportunity to do His work. It is an auspicious beginning for our pilgrimage." It was a pleasure to give Dame Joan a taste of her own piety. And I knew she couldn't refute this argument; she'd so often lectured me about doing God's work.

"Very well," she said. "But I don't like it!"

"Neither do I," said Sir Howard. "Sir Bohemund wouldn't have liked it either."

"My husband would have wished me to do what was right, to help a soul in need."

Sir Howard bowed his head.

"No doubt this creature will slit our throats come evening," Dame Joan continued her complaint. "I know what sort of fiends haunt the king's forest."

"Peace," I said. "I'll hear no more on it."

All the while we debated her fate, Rhiannon kept

still, her eyes on me. She must have let other travelers pass by, others who might have used her ill. As Dame Joan so often said, "These are godless times." Somehow Rhiannon knew to wait for me. Maybe she *was* a witch, and she'd seen me coming to rescue her all the way from Cheswick before I even knew I was leaving it.

"Milady," said Sir Howard, "we had better move along; Godstone is still a ways off."

Yes. I could agree with that. "Let us start at once. The girl will ride with me."

"No!" said Dame Joan. "She'll infest you!"

"Nonsense," I said, and nodded to Rhiannon. She climbed onto the mare, settling herself in front of me, so delicately the horse didn't flinch. How did she manage that so gracefully?

Rhiannon could have ridden in the cart. Dame Joan was probably right about her carrying a goodly assortment of vermin. But I'd not mind the lice and fleas. I wanted to find out more about Rhiannon to help me understand why I was so attracted to her. Other than revealing her name and asking for help, she hadn't spoken a word. Maybe that was what unsettled Dame Joan more than the filth. To our many questions, she'd only shake her head. Why didn't she speak? Her few words, asking for help, had been clearly spoken, if with an odd lilt to them. Did she not understand us? None of us knew how to speak Welsh, but we'd tried

English, Latin, and French. Did she not hear us? And yet, she seemed to know all that transpired. She must have had her reasons for remaining mute.

With Rhiannon nestled against me we proceeded through the forest, then back again to the open road and the bright cold day.

"Won't you please talk to me?" I whispered so as not to attract Dame Joan's attention.

Rhiannon's only reply was to snuggle against me, pulling my cloak more tightly around us both. I hardly noticed any of the country or villages we passed, I was so taken up with her. How old was she? She was slight as a child, but there was something about her that made me wonder if she wasn't my age, or older. Where was she going? Had she come all the way from Wales? Was she trying to get back there, or to get as far from it as possible?

"How long have you been in the king's forest?" In vain I questioned her.

Her clothes were layer upon layer of filthy shreds. They were so ragged and dirty I couldn't tell if they'd once been a noble girl's fine cloak and gown or the coarse garb of a peasant. Was she hiding in the forest from some terrible fate? Was she, as Dame Joan probably suspected, guilty of some crime? The forest was a haven for outlaws. Or, perhaps her home was one of the many destroyed during the war. Sometimes manors and whole villages were obliterated by the battling forces of Empress Matilda or King Stephen. The nobles fought, the people suffered. Maybe she couldn't trust me with her story, yet. I'd try to be patient and wait for her telling.

We stopped when the sun was high to rest the horses on the bank of a fast-running stream. Dame Joan set out bread, cheese, meat pies, and wine on a clean linen cloth. Rhiannon fell upon the food.

"She's eating it all!" said Dame Joan.

"She's hungry," I said. "Perhaps she's not eaten in a long time. Let her have her fill."

"Disgusting!" said Dame Joan, watching Rhiannon shove chunks of bread, cheese, and whole pies into her mouth. "She's eating like a beast!"

"We mustn't judge her," I said. I might have added that it was God's business to judge, but that would be going a little too far. Dame Joan was already sorely tried.

After Rhiannon had eaten her fill, which was all the food Dame Joan had set out, she fell fast and deep into sleep. I had Sir Howard put her in the cart. Dame Joan begged some bread of the men's rations. We ate that, drank some of the water, and continued on to Godstone.

I began to wonder what Brother Simon, my brother, would think of Rhiannon. Four and half years ago, when we were children at Wallingford, he would have been as taken with Rhiannon as I. But perhaps the cloister had changed him. I hoped not. I needed Simon as he had been.

The countryside began to look too much like what we'd already passed: newly plowed winter fields, here a manor house, there a village with a small parish church, or a stand of trees. Once I saw a great castle rising out of the stone walls ringing the crest of a hill. That was a grand sight, but too soon gone. My back ached, my bottom was sore. The ever-present heaviness sat on my chest, choking off the good, cold spring air.

This was only the first day of the journey that might take many months. Our plan was to be in Jerusalem by late summer. Would it all be saddle sores and dull fields? No, soon enough we'd be leaving England; then everything would be different. If I could breathe easily and see something new each day, I'd not mind the aches and pains of travel. But what about Dame Joan? She must be twice as weary as I. Could she endure a year's journeying? And Rhiannon? She looked so frail. How would she fare? I'd have to make her understand my plans and get her clear consent. Getting to Jerusalem had its perils. Brigands plagued the roads, and pirates the seas. I wasn't afraid for myself. If swift Death was waiting on my journey, so be it. At least I wouldn't suffocate in England.

We arrived at Godstone during the prayers for Vespers. Only the ancient monk gatekeeper, bowing low, and some lay brothers were there to greet us. Godstone was like Woburn Abbey only grander, and bigger than Cheswick village and manor combined. The chapel and surrounding buildings were made of a fine honey-colored stone. The gatehouse was turreted, and its huge oaken doors were bound with iron bands. Over the past four years Simon had sent me wonderful drawings of Godstone, full of details, such as the blacksmith's spotted dog, the beehives, and the lay brothers hoeing rows of turnips in the garden. Arriving for the first time, I felt I already knew it.

Peter brought my chest and Dame Joan's to the guest house. Then I sent him to help the men stable the horses, and to tidy himself for our dinner with the abbot.

Once he'd gone, Dame Joan took charge, commanding the lay brothers to bring a tub and buckets of hot water into the closet off our small chamber.

"I'll get the creature clean," she said, "before Abbot Bernard sees her, lest he think we've betrayed his hospitality."

"Abbot Bernard is a holy man," I said. "Surely he'd see beyond a layer of dirt."

"Hmph!"

I nodded to Rhiannon to go with Dame Joan. My old nettle might take more kindly to the girl once she was clean, but I wanted no part of it. I stayed in the chamber, brushing the dirt from my own skirts and putting on a fresh wimple in honor of the abbot.

Rhiannon did not go gently to the bath. I heard her growling, the sounds of scuffling and a great deal of splashing. Once Dame Joan shrieked, "The vixen!" Then came a loud slap, followed by muttering about ungrateful creatures who ought not to *bite* the hand that cares for them.

I had to bite my own lip to keep from giggling.

Eventually Dame Joan emerged, damp and very red in the face, but triumphant. Behind her came Rhiannon. Had she not already captured my heart she would have done so in that moment. She looked so pathetic, and yet so fiercely proud. She stood, shivering, wrapped in a damp cloth that barely covered her. Her dripping hair clung to her head, emphasizing its smallness. Without all her rags and debris, she looked half as big as she had in the forest, although I could see she was more woman than child. Her hair was as dark as my own, nearly black, but her skin was milk white, bluish around her eyes. Her arms and the thin bones of her feet looked so terribly fragile. All I wanted was to gather her in my arms and protect her. Yet she stood straight and dauntless as a knight. As much as I ached to hold her, I knew to let her be. Rhiannon wasn't a poppet for me to cuddle.

I dressed her in my blue gown, the color of her eyes, though Dame Joan had plenty to say against it. The bodice that fit me so neatly, hung like a sack on her. On Rhiannon, my long graceful sleeves, of the new style, dragged along the ground.

"Dear, dear," Dame Joan clucked around her. "It won't do."

"We can sew a seam up the back," I said, "trim and knot the sleeves."

"That will ruin your gown!"

Rhiannon was fingering the silken folds of the gown; a smile lit her face.

"I don't mind," I said. I did mind a bit. The gown was the clear blue of an April sky. Sir Bohemund had said that I looked as noble as a queen in that gown. Even when his eyes had dimmed, he'd notice its blue color. "My little queen," he'd say and kiss my hand.

Rhiannon came forward, took my hand, and lightly kissed it.

"Get out your scissors, Dame Joan," I said. "We haven't much time."

Dame Joan went to do my bidding, every ounce of her considerable self bristling with resentment.

Rhiannon smiled for me alone to see, and mouthed the words, "Thank you."

III.
Brother Simon

Lay brothers escorted us to the private apartment of Abbot Bernard. There were several monks, including the abbot, but I didn't see Simon among them.

"*Benedicite*, Father," I said, sinking to my knees as was suitable in the cloister. Dame Joan curtsied, and Sir Howard bowed beside me. Rhiannon stood stiffly to one side.

"*Benedicite*, my child," said Abbot Bernard, and bid me rise.

"Sir Howard," I said, "Seneschal of Cheswick Manor."

The abbot signed the cross in benediction.

"And this is Dame Joan, my —" I was about to say "nurse," but stopped myself. I was no longer Dame Joan's charge, whatever the old scold might say.

She was looking up at Abbot Bernard, blushing like a young girl. The abbot took her hand to help her stand.

"My companion," I added lamely.

"Welcome." He greeted them both.

"This is Rhiannon." As I beckoned, Rhiannon came next to me and held tightly to my hand, without the slightest obeisance to Abbot Bernard. He studied her, looking both stern and curious.

"We found Rhiannon in the king's forest on our way here. She was like a wild creature."

"Still is," said Dame Joan, and sniffed.

Rhiannon didn't look at all wild now. Dressed in the blue gown and matching pelisse lined with silvery fur, her hair in neat plaits held back with a silver band, she was as noble as a countess. I stood up straighter and smoothed the skirt of my crimson gown to match her bearing.

"How came you to be in the forest?" Abbot Bernard asked her.

She looked calmly at him without answering.

"She asked for help, and revealed her name," I said, "but has said nothing else." I'd decided to keep Rhiannon's "Thank you" to myself.

Abbot Bernard nodded gravely.

"You are all welcome here," he said.

"Thank you for your hospitality," I said. "You do me much honor."

"We are honored to receive the Lady Edith of Cheswick, noble pilgrim and sister of our most promising illuminator."

"Where *is* my brother?" I asked, looking toward the door for his arrival.

Abbot Bernard smiled broadly, and I felt the impertinence of my question. Patience! I shouldn't have demanded Simon; he would show up in due course.

"But he's here," said the abbot.

A tall, dark young friar stepped forward. Could this serious-looking youth with downcast eyes be Simon? As I watched him, the young friar raised his eyes to meet mine. Yes, the mischievous glint was still there. Older, taller, more a man, but still my little brother.

"Simon!" I wanted to embrace him, but "Brother Simon" I dared not.

"Lady Edith," he said, laughing, and took my hand.

Peter arrived with two lay brothers, carrying ewers of warm, scented water, basins in which to wash our hands, and cloths to dry them. Abbot Bernard led us to our places at the trestle table swathed in snowy linen. I was placed at the abbot's right, and Simon on his left. More lay brothers came, carrying steaming platters. I looked down the table to Rhiannon, who sat demurely by Dame Joan. I wondered how she'd comport herself with the food in front of her.

She remained composed while Abbot Bernard blessed the food, though she didn't bow her head, which made me wonder.

Once we began eating, the abbot made polite inquiries about our journey from Cheswick. I was so interested in what Rhiannon might do, I paid little heed to what was being said. When he spoke of "the glory of holy pilgrimage," followed by "thy good father," I concentrated completely on Rhiannon. She was eating with the grace and delicacy of anyone used to dining at a lord's table. I'm not sure if it surprised me, but I could see Dame Joan was completely taken aback. Rhiannon looked so assured and comfortable, it seemed she must be of noble blood. Now I was more curious about her than ever. Suddenly, she looked up at me, alarm written on her face. What troubled her? Had the abbot said something?

"Does that suit you?" the abbot asked me.

I turned to him. What had he been saying? How should I answer him?

"That sounds most generous. Doesn't it, Lady Edith?" said Simon.

"Yes, indeed," I said, following his lead. "It is very kind of you, Father."

I nodded, and expressed more gratitude for being able to travel under Godstone's protection. Traveling with the holy brothers offered the most safety in these warring times. Even the Earl of Essex wouldn't waylay holy men on holy business. It also saved me from hiring a guard. The few men I knew and trusted, my husband's knights and my father's, couldn't be spared to shepherd me to Jerusalem. Both Cheswick and Wallingford needed every fighting man they had. It was a stroke of luck, "a miracle," said Dame Joan, that Abbot Bernard had decided to send a deputation to

Pope Lucius at the very time I was looking for a way to leave England.

"At least we'll all be together for a week," said Abbot Bernard. "Do you leave the girl with us for our sister house in Iffley, Lady Edith, or will you take her to Woburn Abbey?"

Rhiannon gasped and I, alone, heard her unvoiced scream. Her face had gone white with terror.

"Rhiannon will come with me," I said.

"Lady Edith, do you think that wise?"

Obviously the abbot didn't think it. I glanced at Simon to see if he could help me. Simon held his hands as if in prayer, and gazed heavenward.

"I believe Rhiannon was given to my care, and that it is part of His plan," I said, meeting the abbot's severe look. Rhiannon had come to me. I needed her help as she needed mine. I'd not betray her. She would not be shut up in a cloister to scour stone floors and bleach linen.

"The Lord works in mysterious ways, Lady Edith," said Abbot Bernard. "But I caution you that the Devil is also at work in the world." And he looked meaningfully at Rhiannon.

"Amen!" said Dame Joan, her chins bobbing in agreement.

Rhiannon's eyes met mine, and in them I saw her thanks. A smile flickered across Simon's face.

"Your concern, Father, is too kind," I said, and popped a morsel of carp in my mouth, hoping to end this conversation. Yet I knew I'd hear much more about it from Dame Joan.

"Then, a week from today, Tuesday next it is," said the abbot, returning to more neutral ground. "I'd hoped to keep you longer, but the message from your father seems to add some urgency to your leave-taking."

"I beg your pardon," I said, feeling my blood quicken. "What message?"

"The one I mentioned earlier."

Was that what Rhiannon had heard before?

"Your father sent word that King Stephen has agreed to your marriage with Sir Runcival of Surrey."

"No!" Did I whisper or shout it? Now I felt my own terror.

Dame Joan was at my side, patting my hand.

"Mistress, are you all right?"

"We must leave here at once," I said. "I won't be married to Sir Runcival."

"Don't fret, my poplolly," said Dame Joan. "Not even the king can move so quickly."

"You cannot leave sooner than Tuesday," said the abbot. "Your guard won't be ready until then. Besides you are quite safe at Godstone from the machinations of the king."

There was no comfort in that; abbey walls could not keep me safe. My only chance was to be well away from England. But I couldn't go all alone. I had to stay put — and be patient.

The next few days were an agony of fear and waiting. Every time a rider came to Godstone's gate I was sure he'd brought news of my betrothal to that foul-smelling blackguard. Sir Runcival had come once to Cheswick. Once was all my good-hearted husband would tolerate. The thought of being given to him destroyed my sleep. I could not eat — nor breathe.

I concentrated on Rhiannon. Somehow, she kept my fears at bay. She seemed content to be with me, and often followed me about on my restless wanderings like a shadow. Sometimes when I was most plagued by the nasty vision of Sir Runcival, she'd lay a cool hand on mine, and calm me. But she'd not speak. I talked to her constantly, to soothe myself and to entice her to answer me.

"It is a lovely fair day." I'd begin with something bland. "I wish we were on our way, don't you?"

No answer, only her blue-eyed look.

"It looked as if you were running from something. Can't you tell me what it was?"

Nothing.

Had I invented "Help me" and "Thank you"?

"Do you understand that we are going all the way to the Holy Land? It may be very dangerous."

She smiled at that. Why? Because her own journey had already been so full of peril?

"I don't know when I'll return to England. Are you prepared for that?"

She said not a word.

"Would you rather stay in England?"

As often as I asked, she didn't answer. Yet I already had my answer. Rhiannon had chosen me; she'd go where I went, and when she wouldn't I'd know. So I left off pestering her. What did it matter where she came from? Who she was? Would words have changed the bond I felt between us?

Sir Howard left early on Wednesday to return to Cheswick and serve his new master. He bowed deeply before me.

"Godspeed, Sir Howard," I said.

"And to you, mistress," he said. "May your journey be a safe one, and bring you peace."

What did he know of my peace or lack of it?

"Thank you," I said, barely containing my irritation.

Time crawled during our week at Godstone. As mistress of Cheswick, I'd had so many duties and cares, now I had nothing but the worry that Sir Runcival would come at any moment to claim me as his own. To fill the hours, I followed the monks to chapel throughout the day and night when His praises were sung. I recited the familiar words, yet thought nothing of them. I didn't think that He had much to do with me. I could repeat all that the nuns of Woburn had taught me, but while my lips sang the plainsong, my thoughts flew freely. I tried to concentrate on the adventure ahead, yet too often the specter of Sir Runcival interfered.

When I sprang from my warm bed at the midnight bell for the holy office of Matins, Dame Joan mistook my restlessness for zeal. That wasn't the case; there was nothing else for me to do, and a great need to be doing something.

Dame Joan always came with me, though her poor, old bones suffered in the midnight chill of the chapel. Rhiannon only appeared at Prime, to greet the day, and every evening at Vespers, when Dame Joan made her come.

On Friday, in between Masses, I was wandering in the abbey gardens, searching for some distraction in the sad-looking beds. In a few weeks there'd be flowers and sweet, new green shoots. But winter still held sway. It was a gloomy place. There were high walls all around, and the leaden sky hung oppressively low overhead. I felt so trapped. Yet there was naught to do but be patient. I wished I could, at least, scream.

"Aye!" I shrieked. Something very like a spider brushed against my neck. I whirled around, and there was Simon at the tickling end of a feather.

"You, you . . ." I could pinch an irksome little brother, but not one who'd taken holy orders.

Simon laughed into his sleeve and pulled me over to a secluded section where espaliered pear and quince trees grew in patterns against the wall.

"I've missed you," said Simon.

"And I, you."

"Now that you're here, I feel as if I've sprouted wings and taken flight."

"I don't," I said. "I wish we were on the road, far from Sir Runcival's grasp."

"Sir Runcival cannot marry you without your consent," said Simon. "The church won't allow it."

I had been enough in the world to know that little got in the way of great lords' plans.

"You know what times these are," I said. "Do you think Sir Runcival or King Stephen would scruple over church law, and a widow's wishes?"

King Stephen needed loyal followers and silver. By giving me to Sir Runcival he'd gain a man plus his share of my dower. Simon could give me no happy answer, so I changed the subject.

"Being in a convent again makes me itch. Dame Joan would say I've caught Rhiannon's fleas, but I swear it's the cloister. I can't breathe either."

"I don't think it's the cloister that troubles you so."

"What, if not the cloister?"

Simon shrugged.

"How have *you* stood it here for nearly four years?"

"It's not so bad."

"Not bad! It's stifling, it's so . . . so enclosed. It's . . ."

"It truly is all right," he said. "I've found my place. I wish you could see the scriptorium."

Naturally, women were not allowed in that part of

the abbey. I knew that, but I wanted to see Simon's "place."

"Well, show me," I said.

Simon looked perplexed, then he grinned. "Wait here, I've an idea." He ducked around the corner and out of sight.

I studied the twisted trees until Simon returned, carrying a bundle and looking very pleased.

"Brother Edith," he said, handing me a dark brown cassock, just like his own.

I slipped it on over my gown and pelisse, pulling the cowl over my head so that my face was completely shadowed. Looking out of the dark, smelly tunnel, I felt a rush of giddiness.

"Say something," he said.

"Benedicite."

"Lower," he commanded.

"Benedicite," I said, sounding a bit like a frog.

"That will do." He grinned. "Remember to . . ."

"Say it to any of our 'elders or betters,'" I said. "I know about convent life."

"Indeed. Follow me."

We took a convoluted route to the scriptorium. Simon led me through the quietest byways of the abbey. Occasionally we passed other monks, or lay brothers. Only once did I have to croak out my *"Benedicite."* The whole time I kept my eyes fixed on the hem of Simon's robe. I saw little but the worn, stone flags underfoot.

At length, Simon halted and bade me wait outside

a heavy, carved door. A moment later he pulled me inside.

The scriptorium at Woburn Abbey had been a tiny closet off the Mother Superior's chamber. This was a lofty, elegant room where a dozen desks were placed near three tall windows, so that each scribe had the most light possible.

"Usually, someone's in here working," said Simon. "Abbot Bernard had other tasks for us today."

Tasks Simon had managed to avoid.

"Where is your place?" I asked.

"Here."

Simon took me to a desk set slightly apart from the others, and lifted its clean linen cover. There, on the parchment, was the most magical creature I'd ever seen. A dragon glowing like the gems in a king's crown was twisted round a tall letter "S." All around the margins of the page were twined leaves and flowers. Opposite the dragon was Saint George on a white charger caparisoned in celestial blue with gold filigree.

"Oh, Simon! You did this?"

He nodded.

"And the abbot let you?"

He laughed.

"Yes, he even encouraged it. The books we make here are the main support of the abbey."

"It is exquisite," I said. "Though it's hard to imagine anyone making such magic. You have a gift."

"And this is the place for it."

"Yes, I see."

Only in the safety of the cloister could he pursue his art. No wonder he didn't mind the walls. Inside them Simon was free.

"But, then, why do you journey to Rome?"

"Abbot Bernard has plans for me," said Simon, blushing.

"What?"

"I am to show the pope my work and try to get new commissions for Godstone Abbey. This is a present for His Holiness."

Simon pulled a small Book of Hours from a nearby shelf. Very carefully, I leafed through its pages. Inside were beautiful paintings of men and women at work and play throughout the year. There was so much life in each picture. Tears stung my eyes as I came upon the page for the month of February. Simon had painted our home, Wallingford Manor, with every detail in place. Father and Mother sat in the hall before a roaring fire, listening to a minstrel's tale. Outside were snow-covered fields, and in the middle distance, on the frozen pond, a young girl with wild, dark hair was skating.

"You've gotten it all," I said. "Just the way it was. Just the way I was, too."

Simon smiled. I'm sure the holy fathers often told him about the sin of pride, but Simon had good reason to be proud of his art.

I envied my little brother his place. I missed mine.

IV.
Daughter of Heveydd Hen

Abbot Bernard spent the eve of our departure praising our holy endeavor and exhorting us to beware the dangers of the road. Rhiannon fell asleep on the bench where she sat, only a few minutes after the sermon began. I was aching to follow her example. I wanted to sleep and wake and go before Sir Runcival could entrap me.

"Although you are Holy Pilgrims, recognized by all, yet there will be bandits and other unscrupulous men who may threaten you," said Abbot Bernard with such solemnity that I did my utmost to stifle the yawn that was about to split my face in two.

"But the greatest danger of all," he said, leaning over me so that I saw every pore on his substantial nose, "is to your immortal soul. Lady Edith, your soul is in peril."

Dame Joan looked up from stitching the crosses on our cloaks that would mark us as pilgrims, her face wrinkled in worry. Did she think that, too? I shivered.

"The road to Rome and Jerusalem is filled with temptations," continued Abbot Bernard. "Splendor and luxury beyond your imagining will entice you from your true path. Do not be misled!"

This last was directed at Simon, who looked up with round innocent eyes. He wasn't fazed by the abbot, so why was I?

I wished the bell for Compline would ring.

"That which is wicked may seem godly . . ."

It was two to three days' journey to Dover, then the channel crossing. If we could find a boat, if the winds were fair, that might take only a day. Then I'd be in Boulogne and safe. After that would come Paris, the whole unknown length of France to Marseille, a boat to the port nearest Rome — the great pagan city, the holy city of the pope. From there we'd travel to the port of Bari, to another ship, and then to Jerusalem! The beautiful world lay ahead of me, if I could escape from England, and if I could survive the journey. I didn't mind the risks. I had to go, and I wanted to go. Only in the going would I be free. Only outside of England could I leave behind the stifling weight on my breast.

". . . and that which is good may not appear so."

"Yes!" said Dame Joan, jabbing her needle into the cloak on her lap. "The Devil has many entrapments." She nodded in the direction of Rhiannon, who chanced at that moment to snore loudly.

"Beware of the —"

Ding, Ding, Dong.

Finally, the bell for Compline. Abbot Bernard's sermon was over. We woke Rhiannon and walked in merciful silence to the church.

Between Matins and Prime all was in an uproar. Dame Joan bullied Peter and the lay brothers who were readying our baggage.

We broke our fast with Simon at the abbot's table directly after Prime. Abbot Bernard's sermonizing was done with. Now his advice was practical, and I listened with care as he repeated his instructions about arranging for the boat at Dover to cross the channel, and how I was to manage my finances on the journey. Naturally, the older monks would be there to advise me, but many decisions were mine to make. I'd brought a chest filled with silver, and Dame Joan had sewn jewels and many pieces of gold and silver into belts which we wore beneath our gowns. But I couldn't carry all the silver I'd need for my journey. It would be too unwieldy and dangerous. Most of the silver for my journey I left in the abbot's care. He would also manage my lands and collect rents, while I was away.

Abbot Bernard had given me letters that I could present at any of the Benedictine houses along our route for whatever I might need. My debts would be repaid by Abbot Bernard when French or Italian clerics came to England. It seemed complicated, but the abbot assured me it would work.

"At the papal court in Rome you can get further advice for arranging about the sea crossing. Once you've reached the far shore, the Templars can help you." Abbot Bernard fell silent.

I got up and knelt before him.

"Thank you, Father, for all your kindness."

He placed his hands on my head, and spoke. "Keep this child from harm. Heal her troubled heart, lead her to your Grace, bring her safely to her journey's end and back again."

His blessing brought me a vision of peace I'd not known for a long, long time. It was a window opening up onto what might be, and it soothed me during the delays and disorder for our going.

Despite his misgivings about Rhiannon, the abbot gave her a handsome present, a fine white horse to ride. I was surprised and pleased. I could tell Rhiannon was, too. When she took her leave of the abbot, she bowed her proud head and kissed his fingertips. Abbot Bernard smiled and blessed her. Dame Joan sniffed loudly. Simon received his blessing and the abbot's embrace. And then we were on our way.

There were four brothers in our company, including Simon, five lay brothers, three armed yeomen who owed service to Godstone Abbey, and Sir Raymond d'Aubin of France with his two men. We'd had to await Sir Raymond's arrival from York, which is what had kept us so long at Godstone. He'd been hired by

Abbot Bernard as an extra precaution. Most pilgrims didn't travel with an armed guard. Simon said that the abbot wanted us to make as fine a showing as possible in Rome. Sir Raymond certainly looked the part. He was a broad, swarthy man. Atop his huge bay warhorse, he seemed even more formidable. Although I'd resented the delay he'd caused, I could see the use in having a fighting man in our midst. Yet, how much would this stranger risk on my behalf?

With Dame Joan, Rhiannon, Peter, and me, we were nineteen souls. Too many, I thought, but there was little I could say about it. The brothers, lay brothers, and the yeomen walked. Peter and one of the lay brothers drove the cart that would be sent back to Godstone once we'd arranged our passage at Dover. We'd buy a new cart and a cart horse in Boulogne. The riding horses would make the channel crossing with us. It would be cheaper to send them back to Godstone and buy new mounts in France, but Abbot Bernard advised keeping them and I agreed. I loved my little horse, and well she served me. I'd not like to have to ride a stranger all the long road ahead.

I had thought that once we'd left Godstone and were in the open air Rhiannon might talk to me. Perhaps the walls of the cloister had kept her mute. We rode side by side, and I tried to coax a word from her by chattering about the road ahead, and the weather, until Rhiannon's look silenced me. My noise brought us no closer to friendship. I'd have to wait for her to let me step closer to her heart.

It was also difficult to speak with Simon. The older monks, Brothers Eustace, Aldobert, and John, wouldn't allow him to "engage in idle prattle." Yet I noticed that Brother Eustace walked willingly at Dame Joan's side, chatting about all that we passed. Once Dame Joan and Brother Eustace started gossiping, it was easier for me to slip to the end of the line where Simon dawdled. Rhiannon always came with me. I could tell she liked listening to Simon just by the way she'd cock her head to one side while studying some distant speck.

On the morning of our second day's journey out of Godstone, Rhiannon and I had fallen back to the end of the line while Dame Joan distracted Brother Eustace, and Brothers Aldobert and John were praying over their beads.

"I wish we were already in Dover," I said.

"I wish we could stop at London," said Simon. "It's so like a grand fair."

"You've been to London?"

"Only twice." He sighed.

"Only *twice!* I've never been to London. I thought you were kept shut up in the cloister."

"Father Abbot sent me out into the world to see its glories," said Simon, "and to the scriptoriums of other monasteries, that I might learn from their work."

"And I've been feeling sorry for you all this time," I said. "Where else have you been, besides London?"

"To Durham and Canterbury cathedrals, and I've seen the great chalk horse in Uffington."

"What?"

"Carved into the hillside of chalk is the outline of a horse bigger by far than Oxford Castle."

"No! It cannot be."

"Yes, I swear it's true."

I noticed that Rhiannon was no longer feigning indifference. In fact, she leaned toward Simon, her eyes wide and bright.

"Who could make such a thing?" I asked. It didn't make any sense to me, a horse bigger than Oxford Castle!

Simon looked around, making sure the brothers weren't about to pounce. He lowered his voice to the merest breath. "The ancients did it, before."

"Before what?" I was growing impatient.

"Hush," he said.

"Before what?" I demanded.

"Before Christ," whispered Rhiannon, and her face glowed.

"You've spoken!"

Her look was disdainful.

"But you've not said anything since first we found you."

Her only response was a sniff of irritation. I was rushing her, and I'd have to wait.

"Do you know it?" asked Simon. His eyes were as bright as hers.

"I have seen it with my own eyes," said Rhiannon.

Again she spoke! This time I could hear the music of a different language in her voice, though her words were quite clear. Only why didn't she speak to me?

"Why are you both so enchanted with a horse on a hillside?"

"Because," said Rhiannon, "before Christ, before the Roman gods, my people worshiped the horse."

"Your people, the Welsh?" I asked.

"Of course," she said.

"Have you also seen the Standing Stones on Salisbury Plain?" Simon asked her.

"Yes," she said. "And they are most wondrous!"

"Stones?" I said, growing more irritated.

"There are stones, like giants," said Simon. "They stand in a great circle. The ancients studied there the stars."

"The Romans' stones?" I asked.

"No, no," said Rhiannon. "This was also before the invaders, even before the Druids."

"Pagans, stones, can you not tell me anything of Rhiannon?"

"Very well," she said, with a teasing smile. "I will tell you Rhiannon's tale."

Finally, I'd hear her story.

"Once Pwyll, Prince of Dyved, saw a lady wondrous

fair, dressed in shining gold, and riding upon a great white horse," began Rhiannon.

"Is this a Welsh tale?" I asked.

Rhiannon glared at me.

Of course it was.

"All right, I'll be quiet."

"Prince Pwyll sent one of his men to inquire of the lady. Although it seemed the lady's horse walked quite slowly, and though Pwyll's man ran as fast as he could, he could not catch up with her."

Rhiannon's eyes danced. Simon, too, seemed delighted with this tale. But I grew impatient. What did this have to do with the girl in front of me?

"So it went for three days," said Rhiannon. "Prince Pwyll's men pursued the lady on the swiftest of horses, but they could not overtake her."

I cared not for the tale, but Rhiannon's voice was mesmerizing.

"At last," she continued, "the prince went out on his own noble steed to meet the lady. She stopped immediately to greet him. And this is what she said: 'I am Rhiannon, daughter of Heveydd Hen.'"

"And is that you" I asked.

Rhiannon glared at me. "This tale is for *you*," she said. "Just listen."

Rhiannon continued her story. "'A husband has been chosen for me,' said Rhiannon, daughter of Heveydd Hen, 'but I won't have him. The only man

I'll wed is you, Pwyll. And I have come to hear your answer.'"

"That's enough!" I cried. "I'll hear no more of this. It's not decent."

Both Simon and Rhiannon looked at *me* as if I were crazy. I wasn't crazy, I just . . . I wanted to know about the Rhiannon who was right before my eyes. I didn't want to hear about this bold woman choosing her own husband. I couldn't bear it.

"Listen to yourself," said Simon.

"You sound like Old Wobbly Chins," said Rhiannon.

"I do *not* sound like Dame Joan!" I said.

"Brother Simon!" called Brother Aldobert, sharply. "Walk with Brother John and me. Or the Devil will catch you by your careless tongue."

Simon shrugged and caught up with the monks. Rhiannon shot me a look, then took her horse to a place in line behind Dame Joan. Did she, then, prefer the company of Old Wobbly Chins to me?

I remained at the back of the line with the yeomen. Anger grew in me, and I couldn't tell if I was more angry at the girl or myself. Why did she have to be such a puzzle? Why was she telling me tales of a Welsh wanton?

The men began singing a rude song. It was up to me to correct them, or say something to Sir Raymond.

I spurred my mare. At least I could get away from them. I'd go right to Sir Raymond. It was his duty to manage the men.

As I rode past Rhiannon, she reached out an arm to stay me. I reined in my horse.

"Yes?" I asked.

She smiled at me.

"Did you want something?"

She only smiled in reply.

"You haven't a word to spare me? And I thought we could be friends."

"We can be friends," she said. "When you give up the idea of owning me. I belong only to myself."

"But I . . . I don't want to own you," I stammered. "I only want . . ." Yet when I stopped a moment to think, I realized she was right. I wanted to understand her completely; I wanted to know all about her, to possess her. She was my wild creature and no other's. I sighed. Was I as bad as Sir Runcival? Perhaps it was all wrong. I shouldn't be taking Rhiannon with me. I should have left her in Godstone.

"No!" she said. "Do not think such a thing."

"What!"

"I was meant to go with you," she said.

"You heard my thoughts." I felt a tingle of excitement and fear. "How?"

"It cannot be explained," said Rhiannon. "And I do not always know what you are thinking. For instance, why were you riding past me just now so full of purpose?"

"I was on my way to tell Sir Raymond that the men were singing a rude song."

"You were?" Her eyes were merry.

In that moment I knew what she was thinking. Taking offense at the men's song was Dame Joan's province, not mine. I was not a sanctimonious old woman, not yet. I looked at Rhiannon's mischievous grin.

"No," I said.

And we both laughed.

V.
Channel Crossing

It took us three days to reach Dover. We stayed in one verminous inn, and the guest house of St. Colomba's Convent in Kent. When my bottom got too sore from the saddle, I'd slip off my horse and walk along with Simon. It felt good to stretch my legs, and have some moments alone with him. Rhiannon never dismounted. I think she might have slept on her palfrey if we'd let her. I wondered if her people still worshiped the horse.

There was no sign of Sir Runcival or his men. I began to hope that Dame Joan and the abbot were right, that I would be well away before he could track me down.

When Dame Joan wasn't around to hear, Rhiannon spoke to me and Simon, but she'd never answer any of my questions about her past. She and Simon talked of distant times and places, of heroes and heroines I'd never heard of. How did she know such things? Simon had access to Godstone's library, but how could Rhiannon be so learned? It certainly wasn't anything taught in a convent. Was this what Welsh girls learned? Or had she been educated in some other place?

The tales of old were fascinating, but I was more interested in the mysteries before my very nose.

"I still don't understand why you won't tell me who you are, and where you're from," I said to Rhiannon.

"I'll tell you my story when you tell me all of yours," she said.

"That's nonsense," I said. "I've already told you everything."

"Ha!" said Rhiannon.

"What else is there? I left Wallingford, married Sir Bohemund, and decided to go on this pilgrimage when he died, before I could be married off again."

"What else is there?" she echoed. "The most important part. The part you're *not* telling. The heart of the matter, Lady Edith."

What was I not telling? What was the "heart of the matter"? Was it the babe? Perhaps. I didn't want to talk about her. I felt as if there was something else, as well — a piece of my story gone missing. Only I knew not what.

Meanwhile Rhiannon hadn't told me anything about herself.

"At least tell me how old you are," I said.

"How old do you think?"

"I think you might be almost as old as I am," I said.

"Oh, I'll never be that old," she said.

I didn't speak to her for some time after that. I rode by Dame Joan's side, taking comfort in her prattle. But I couldn't be angry with Rhiannon for long.

The road took us past green hills and brown fields, and though it was new, nothing was different from what I'd already known — until we came to the sea. First, the air grew heavier, filled with wetness and a briny smell. White and gray sea birds wheeled overhead, complaining harshly. The road rose steadily; at its crest the earth suddenly fell away. At first it looked as if the land had disappeared altogether and nothing was left but gray sky. Then I saw that the lower part of the sky was a great restless heaving, and that was the sea.

Rhiannon leapt from her horse and ran pell-mell down the steep path. The rest of us dismounted and followed much more carefully. The men led the horses. Brother Eustace helped Dame Joan, and I was glad of Simon's arm as we edged down to the strand. Dame Joan and the others stayed back against the rising white cliffs, while Simon and I ventured close to where the water broke on the rocky shore. That's where Rhiannon was. She'd shed her shoes and stockings and was chasing the incoming water, laughing when it caught her. Already her skirts were sodden and her hair tangled by the salt wind.

"Run with me," she said.

Simon shook his head. I'm sure he would have if it weren't for the disapproving brothers.

"You come," Rhiannon caught my hand, pulling me with her a few steps.

"Nay, I'll watch you," I said. I wasn't even tempted. Running barefoot was no longer for me.

"Lazy-bones," she teased, twirling away from me.

Simon and I stood by the sea without speaking. Perhaps he was trying to measure its vastness with his artist's eye. I was content to watch Rhiannon and the surging water. It was a bit frightening to see all that emptiness, with not a speck of green growing. The winds blustered. The birds shrieked. The sea flung itself upon the shore, backed away, and came again. Over and over. Its "shush, shush" sound filled my head. Waves, I thought, and for the first time the word had meaning. The constant ebb and flow began to lull me. It was so like a cradle always rocking — always rocking. I never let anyone else tend the babe's cradle because I wanted to be the one to set it gently rocking. I loved to watch her. She'd stare back at me with eyes like dark stars. Slowly, as I rocked, her eyes would soften, and her eyelids flutter and shut as sleep took her. I could have stared at her forever.

"Mistress!"

It was Peter. Peter the messenger, calling me back to my duties. His eyes were bright, his nose and cheeks reddened from the sea winds.

"Yes, yes," I said, trying to come back to the present, to Dover. Peter needn't say a word. I knew it was time to seek out our lodging at the priory of St. Martin's-le-Grand. It was time to look for a ship. It was time to be leaving England while I could. This was not the moment for standing dumbstruck before the sea.

"Rhiannon!" I called.

St. Martin's-le-Grand was large and well prepared for visitors. Many came. Travelers bound for Canterbury cathedral, merchants on their way to the continent, clerks going to study in Paris, pilgrims and fugitives — all stayed here. The guest house was large and clean, but very crowded. Sir Raymond and the yeomen went to the men's quarters. Simon and the brothers were enfolded into the cloister. I saw Simon only at meals. Godstone was the priory's brother house, and so we had special favor, and dined at the abbot's table. Otherwise, we'd have supped on coarse bread and milk with the other travelers.

At night Dame Joan and I were lucky to have a cot to share; Rhiannon had a pallet on the rushes. The room was wide but so full of sleepers it was as stuffy and rank as a dovecote. Those around me seemed lost in heavy breathing sleep. Sleep was beyond my grasp. I was wide awake and suffocating. I crept from our cot, stepping with care around the bundled forms of dreaming strangers, to the window.

I wrenched open the shutter. In came a welcome gust of salt air. The cold felt wonderful. High in the night sky was the full-faced moon. A wavery line of silver moonlight stretched across the water between me and Boulogne. In France I'd be safe. I'd be free and able to breathe. Perhaps on the morrow we'd find our ship and could set out. The sound of the ceaseless sea began to calm me. My heart stopped racing; the heaviness of sleep was on me. I tiptoed back to my cot and was glad to burrow next to the snoring warmth of Dame Joan.

"Better now?" asked Rhiannon from the dark beside me.

"Yes," I whispered.

"Today, on the shore, what did you see?" she asked.

"Nothing," I said. "I saw the waves."

"Only that?"

"Only that."

Early the next day, Dame Joan, Peter, and I marched down from the Western Heights, through the tightly packed streets of Dover to the quay to find a ship. We didn't have much to choose from. There were only three vessels in the harbor. The first two boats were quite small. It was easy to see why their captains refused to take the horses. That left us with the *Sea Spray.* It seemed big enough to carry the horses if it could carry anything without sinking. I knew nothing about boats, but even I could tell that this one was in a sorry state. The rigging looked like one big knot, the canvas was green with mildew, and the big belly of the hull was crusted with barnacles and slimed with seaweed. And the stink of it! As anxious as I was to leave England, setting sail in the *Sea Spray* was a gloomy prospect. Undaunted, Dame Joan commenced to bargain with the evil-eyed captain.

"Aye," he said. "I'll take the horses on, but it's a tricky business. And you've got a warhorse, you say?"

"Yes," said Dame Joan. "A destrier and three palfreys."

"It will cost you dear," he said, and asked for a fortune in silver.

"That's an impossible price!" said Dame Joan. "I shall report you to the port guards."

"Now, surely we can come to some understanding," he said, leering at me.

I was useless at this sort of business. Better for me to keep silent beside Peter and let Dame Joan handle it. If she couldn't manage the captain, no one could.

"Seeing as how you are fine ladies," said the captain, "and it will be an honor and pleasure to offer you safe passage, I'll consider a reduction in my price."

"Do that," said Dame Joan. "We'll not pay a penny more than the rates established by the port guards."

"But those rates don't account for warhorses!"

"Then we shall take passage on another vessel."

Surely the captain knew we wouldn't do that. We had to take this ship. Other ships might be available soon, but I couldn't wait. Of course, the captain didn't know that. He continued ogling me, his oily grin unchanged.

"Perhaps there can be some accommodation," he said at last.

"Come, Lady Edith," said Dame Joan.

Before I knew what she was about, she turned and marched briskly down the gangplank, and away toward town. The captain looked as startled as I was. Without taking his leave, I grabbed Peter and hurried after her.

She was panting when I caught up with her on the quay, but she didn't slow down.

"What are you doing?" I asked. "We've got to get on that ship."

"Don't worry," she said. "We will. Are they following?"

I started to turn, and she caught my arm.

"Just peek," she said. "Don't let them see you."

"Someone's coming," I said.

"Good!" She was breathless, but as jolly as ever I'd seen her. "Now . . . we've . . . got . . . him!"

"Please, settle the business," I begged. "I don't care what it costs."

"You'll not give that pirate a penny more than what's right," she said.

"Mistress," called the ship's boy.

I tried to stop, but Dame Joan pulled me onward. The poor boy didn't catch up with us until we were far beyond the quay and into the heart of Dover. Dame Joan was so red in the face, I thought she'd faint. I was breathless, too, and fretful that I was losing my chance to escape.

"Mistress, please!" said the boy. "My master says he'll accept your terms."

Dame Joan put on a grave face and nodded.

"Will you, please, talk to my master?"

Please, I thought.

"Certainly," she said. "He may come to the priory of St. Martin's-le-Grand on the morrow."

"Mistress, couldn't you, please, come back to the ship?"

"Of course not," said Dame Joan.

The boy sighed deeply and went off to face his master's wrath.

Once he was out of earshot, Dame Joan grabbed my arm and cackled. "You see how it's done?"

It was well done. She'd gotten us a ship for a good price. But I felt sorry for the ship's boy, and myself. If Dame Joan weren't so clever we might have been on our way to France. Now there'd be another day's delay. Another day for Sir Runcival to find me.

The *Sea Spray*'s captain came the next day. He agreed to all of Dame Joan's terms, and this time there was no ogling, no sly grin. He left with half a purse of silver in a fit of temper. Dame Joan couldn't have been more pleased. I was glad to have the business settled, and the journey not further delayed. If the winds were good on the morrow we'd set sail. With any luck, we'd make the crossing to Boulogne in half a day.

The winds were not fair. For five interminable days we waited. The ship's boy came banging on the gate of the priory of St. Martin's-le-Grand near midnight of our sixth day in Dover.

"Master says the winds will be right by morning," he said. "He wishes you on board within the hour."

What a scramble trying to get ready! Somehow Dame Joan managed it. Rhiannon and I merely did our best to keep out of her way.

The service for Matins was just beginning as we left the priory and stumbled down the darkened streets to the quay, and the waiting *Sea Spray.*

The horses were already aboard, and not happy about it. I wondered if Sir Raymond's destrier might not kick the boat to pieces. All of our things were stowed below. The captain sent the women and monks down the hatch as well, to keep us out of the way of the sailors. Sir Raymond and the yeomen stayed aloft, for no one was likely to bully them into the stinking hold.

We perched on our chests and the barrels filling the cramped space and waited. It seemed an hour passed, maybe more. There was the constant rumble and stamp of the men readying the ship above us. Even at rest in the calm harbor, the heaving of the ship was starting to make me queasy. The ship's boy scampered down the ladder, and dropped a bucket at my feet.

"What this?" I asked.

"'Tis for your puking," he said and darted back up to the air.

My stomach lurched. By now the rocking of the sea had truly lost its charm. We'd be stuck in this wretched place for the rest of the night and all the long day ahead of us whilst crossing the channel. Dame Joan looked quite green.

"If Sir knight gets to stay on deck, we should, too," Rhiannon whispered in my ear. "Look at Dame Joan. She's going to puke now, and we haven't even left the harbor."

Simon and the other monks looked at me as if I should do something. They were right. It was up to me.

I gathered my skirts, and climbed the ladder, with Peter at my heels. I summoned the ship's boy; I'd start with someone easy to order about, and work up to the captain.

"Tell the captain I wish to speak with him," I said. I clasped my hands tightly to keep their trembling from betraying me.

"Yes, milady."

Presently the captain appeared, all snarls and impatience.

“We cannot stay in the hold,” I said, trying to sound as if I were in charge. “You will make space for all of us on the deck, or return our silver.”

I saw him ready to tear me apart, and knew I had to keep going forward.

“Sir Raymond,” I called. And my hearty knight lumbered to my side.

“Milady.”

“Please have one of the men carry Dame Joan onto the deck. She is indisposed.”

This was the first time I’d spoken directly to Sir Raymond. I saw him hesitate, deciding if I was, indeed, his mistress. The captain saw that hesitation, too, for his eyes lit up with triumph.

In a moment Sir Raymond decided in my favor. “As you wish, milady,” he said, and sent two men to heft Dame Joan up the ladder. He stayed at my side, presenting a fine obstacle to any objection the captain might have. Good, Sir Raymond, I thought, my own valorous knight.

“If a storm comes up in the channel, you’ll all be washed away,” growled the captain.

I nodded, trying to look sober, but laughter bubbled up inside me. It was such a heady feeling, getting these two men to obey me. Somehow I’d done it! I’d taken charge. It was such a surprise; even more that it had worked. I allowed myself a wink in Peter’s direction, which sent him into a fit of giggles.

By first light the anchor was raised. The sailors clambered all over the ship, high up in the rigging, like squirrels chasing about in trees. The captain shouted orders, and men actually hopped to obey him. Ropes were pulled this way and that, and the sails unfurled. The white canvas billowing above us caught the glow of morning and ennobled the *Sea Spray* as she set out into the channel.

We were crowded into a corner of the ship, with the nervous horses. The sailors often had to crawl over and around us to get at the ropes. The discomfort didn't seem to bother any of us. In fact we all were in good spirits. Dame Joan recovered quickly in the air. Even Brother Aldobert lost his usual dour look, and grinned into the wind.

The boat lurched and heaved as it rode great swells, and bounced over choppy waves. Before we reached Boulogne every one of us, except Peter, who was remarkably unaffected, had used the puking bucket. It could have gone much worse. The channel is famous for sudden storms, but we were lucky. I was particularly glad not to give the captain the satisfaction of drowning. Even so, it was a relief to enter the mouth of the Liane River, and wait for the tide to draw us into Boulogne harbor.

"Imagine, if we'd had to stay in that filthy hold the whole way," said Dame Joan as she mopped my brow with a damp cloth. "Peter said you handled the captain better than Sir Bohemund — saved us all a good deal of misery. Well done, my lovey."

Was my old nettle complimenting me?

"I've always said there are some fine uses for your temper."

Not that I could recall.

Simon and Rhiannon were white-faced, but otherwise well. Only Brother John still hovered over the puking bucket.

Ahead, my adventure awaited. Ahead of us was France!

VI.
Bertrade de Montfort

It wasn't at all as I'd hoped, once we'd crossed the channel. I still didn't feel free; I didn't feel safe. We were too close to England. What was to stop Sir Runcival from taking ship across the water after me? If I were a poor widow nobody would bother with me. But if I were poor, I'd be stuck in some closet in England, maybe even forced into a worse match than Sir Runcival. Perhaps my problem was that Boulogne seemed too much like England. The town looked a bit like Dover, without the cliffs. There were too many Normans and Englishmen about. If I could get farther away, where it was truly foreign, then I might lose my worries and myself.

"First we'll go to St. Denis," said Simon. "Abbot Suger's church is said to be a marvel. Everything in it is as fine and rich as possible."

"Beware the sin of luxuriousness," droned Brother Aldobert.

"It is all for the greater glory of God," said Simon, looking angelic, except for the fiendish twitch at the corner of his mouth.

At St. Denis our party would swell. The abbot of St. Martin's-le-Grand had asked if two monks from his abbey, who were already in Anjou, could travel under our protection to Rome. I wanted to refuse him, for it would mean a delay of some days in St. Denis while word was sent to the brothers, and we waited their arrival, but I couldn't. Maybe I'd not mind the waiting so much at St. Denis. It was almost at the walls of Paris. I might have begun to feel less myself by then.

What a wonderment was Abbot Suger's new church! Passing through the gleaming bronze doors, we seemed to have entered the miraculous light of heaven. All the other churches and chapels I'd known were twilight worlds, heavy with incense and dark shadows. St. Denis's soaring nave was more window than wall. And those windows were filled with pictures in colored glass telling Christ's story. They sent down shafts of azure, emerald, crimson, and golden light to pool upon the marble floor.

Walking through cascades of pure color hushed us all. Rhiannon's usual look of disdain for the Church and all its trappings was replaced by awe. Dame Joan was so overtaken she could barely set one foot before the other, and leaned heavily on Brother Eustace. The brothers stumbled about, their heads tilted back to read the brilliant stories in the windows, their mouths agape. Peter, my jolly page, had tears in his eyes. All of our company looked stunned. Even Sir Raymond seemed humbled. Not Simon. His face was a study of perfect delight. His hands reached out to touch the streams of colored light, the spots of blues, greens, and reds tickling his fingers. I was, at first, nearly as struck as Dame Joan. Watching Simon showed me the playful beauty of Abbot Suger's creation, and my heart grew lighter.

On our fifth day at St. Denis, the monks still hadn't arrived from Anjou. Dame Joan and the brothers directed our footsteps to the church every morning upon rising, and here we remained except for a meager noon dinner at the convent, and an even more frugal supper in the evening. I still felt the initial thrill of walking through the heavy doors into the enchantment of color and light. But I was tiring of hour upon hour spent revering the holy. It was past time to be going. I regretted my promise to the abbot in Dover. As each day passed, I felt increasingly certain that Sir Runcival's arrival was imminent. If only we could keep traveling.

Rhiannon was bored and restless as a caged cat.

"I wish we were in Paris," she said. "I would like to see where Peter Abelard preached. I've heard the Louvre is a gloomy old place, but Queen Eleanor has brought with her the sun of Provence."

"How do you know such things?" I asked.

"I have listened," she said, obliquely. "Perhaps we could beg an audience with the queen."

"Of what interest is Lady Edith of Cheswick to Queen Eleanor?"

"None," she said. "But she would be interested in me. And I know she'd want to see Simon's work."

"And why would the queen want to see you?" I asked.

"To inquire of my family," said Rhiannon. Then she said no more. Why would her family be of interest to the Queen of France? Wasn't her family Welsh? Perhaps her mother was French? I didn't understand, and knew Rhiannon wasn't likely to enlighten me. It was maddening how her mysteries multiplied.

Simon still seemed to find much to study and delight in, although he was anxious to get to Paris, the city of scholars. I envied Peter, who stayed in the cloister's kitchen and gardens working with the lay brothers. Perhaps if I had something to do, I wouldn't worry so much about Sir Runcival. Perhaps if I didn't have to spend all my waiting in a church . . .

I'd been denied the comforts of church for sixty-six days after the birth of my babe. A new mother was considered unclean. If my babe had been a boy, I'd have been unclean for only thirty-three days. I didn't care about that. I was secretly glad to have had a daughter — a girl like me. Then, even before my churching, they were both dead, my husband and my little one.

I walked behind my husband's bier to the churchyard, but I could not enter the church to pray for him. Neither could I weep before the Holy Mother for my lost child. During that long time kept from the church, I'd grown used to doing without it. Now it was oppressive to spend so much time inside a church, even this one. I longed for fresh air and the long ride on my mare to Paris. The suffocating heaviness I'd felt so keenly in England had returned. The channel crossing had only brought me temporary relief. If leaving England could not cure me, what would?

On our sixth morning at St. Denis, Rhiannon was especially quiet and sulky. She'd retreated into black-browed silence. I felt the same way, and my head throbbed. I wished she'd tell me something about herself. That would chase away boredom and the pain behind my eyes.

"How joyous to be holy pilgrims setting out in the midst of so many other holy pilgrims starting their great journey," exclaimed Dame Joan.

Was it the hundredth, or thousandth, time she'd said that? Men and women gathered here to begin the pilgrimage to Santiago de Compostela, the sacred shrine of St. James, in Spain. Dame Joan never seemed to tire of remarking upon it.

Simon turned to me and said, "Praise God."

Rhiannon paid no attention to any of us. Dame Joan's piety, Simon's mischievousness, and my own friendship were nothing to her. Nothing that we said, or did, could rouse her from her sullenness. I began to regret bringing her with me. What had so possessed me about the girl that I was carrying her all the way to the Outremer? Perhaps I should send her back to England before we'd gone much further.

Rhiannon stopped suddenly and gave me a fierce look. I'd forgotten, for the moment, that she could read my thoughts.

"I'm sorry," I whispered. "I'm truly worried that bringing you on this journey was wrong. You seem so . . ."

Rhiannon held up her hand to hush me, and held Simon and me back while Dame Joan and the brothers proceeded along the nave. Once they were past, Rhiannon took my hand and walked purposefully to a darkened chapel. Here were buried the kings of France. She stopped in front of the tomb of Philip I, and all the dark moodiness of the past four days left her. Rhiannon's eyes glittered.

"I found something yesterday that concerns you. Now is the moment." Her voice was hushed but bright. She was crackling with excitement. But I couldn't be pleased with this turnaround. Something in her manner frightened me.

"I have a love story to tell," said Rhiannon.

"A love story doesn't concern me," I said.

"It does," she said, and began. "Young Bertrade de Montfort was married to the old Fulks Le Rechin, Count of Anjou. For a time Bertrade lived dutifully and unhappily with her husband. Then one day Philip I, the young king of France, came to Anjou, and stole her heart."

Why did this concern me? I didn't like it. My head hurt so, I wished she'd stop.

"The fair Bertrade would not be parted from her love, nor he from her. They found a bishop who agreed to marry them." Rhiannon folded her arms across her chest, and looked at me, meaningfully.

"I don't want to hear any more of this," I said, holding my head. "What they did was wrong."

"It isn't wrong to choose happiness," said Rhiannon.

"It is," I said. "God would punish them."

"That's what the priests would have you believe," she said.

Simon nodded.

"They tried to punish them. The pope excommunicated Philip, but he would not betray Bertrade."

I could not breathe. The incense was too thick and heady. And it had become unbearably warm in the church. I had to get outside, to some air.

"Finally after twelve years of petitioning and dispute, the Parisian church court granted an annulment to Philip, and ratified Bertrade's divorce. Philip and Bertrade lived happily ever after."

Now both Simon and Rhiannon were looking at me.

"What is it?" They were unnerving me.

"I want to know," said Rhiannon, "who is your Philip?"

"Don't be ridiculous," I said. "I am not a French strumpet. I have no Philip."

"Your crimson cheeks tell a different story," said Rhiannon.

This was nonsense, but it was making me furious. I was never unfaithful to my husband. It was unthinkable. If my cheeks were burning, it wasn't for shame, but because I was so hot.

"I know exactly what I ran from and why," said Rhiannon. "You haven't any idea, have you?"

"I'm not running away from anything, but Sir Runcival of Surrey," I answered.

"And?"

"That is all."

"There's much more," she said. "That is only part of it."

"There is nothing more." I barely had breath to speak; it was so close in this dark corner. What was she implying?

Rhiannon reached out and gently stroked my hand with her cool fingertips. Her blue eyes searched mine.

Then Simon petted my other hand and looked at me as if I were a child.

"Edith does have a Philip, whether she knows it or not," he said. "Her Philip is William Belet."

"I will not hear this!" I said.

"Whether or not you will hear it," said Simon, "I must tell it. Will Belet asks for you in every letter he writes me. You are never far from his thoughts. And I know that once he was always in your thoughts."

I turned to leave them; perhaps I turned too quickly. All I remember was heat and dizziness.

The next thing I knew I was outside the church, lying on a bench in the square. Dame Joan leaned over me, waving a pomander of cardamon and cloves.

"There, there, Poplolly, you're all right now." She petted me and fussed. "What did that little Welsh witch say to you?"

"Nothing," I said. I looked around for Simon and Rhiannon. Dame Joan must have shooed them away. How stupid of me to faint.

"I saw her muttering curses," said Dame Joan. "She doesn't think I notice, but these old eyes see quite well."

"She was only telling a story," I said. It was something about King Philip. What was it? "Why do you call Rhiannon a witch?"

"All those tales she spins about pagans and druids. Hmph!" said Dame Joan. "That girl will one day burn. If Simon isn't careful, he'll be on the pyre with her. So, what was her story?"

"Something about a French king," I said.

"Why should that make you swoon?"

"I don't know," I said, and truly I didn't.

Then I remembered. I'd fainted when Simon had said that Will Belet was my love.

Will Belet was of the time before my marriage, when I was still a girl. I had stopped thinking of him. I'd had to. Rightfully, my heart belonged to my husband. It still did. My eyes filled with tears.

"Lady Edith," said Dame Joan. She wrapped me in her arms, and rocked me like a little baby. And I began to sob.

It was dreadful. Strangers began to crowd around me. I hid my face in Dame Joan's cloak.

"Please take me away from here," I wailed.

"Poor child," she murmured, and wiped my face.

Brothers John and Eustace appeared and helped pull me to my feet.

"We'll take her back to the convent," said Dame Joan. "I'll get the infirmarer to prepare her a draught."

Supported by the brothers, I stumbled back to the guest house of the convent of St. Denis. My head was swimming. Dame Joan put me to bed. Something vile was poured down my throat. And that's the last I knew.

VII.
Possessed

We remained at St. Denis for three weeks. I have hardly any memories of that time. I was lost in the mists of fever and a black dread. Dame Joan was constantly at my side. Whenever I woke from my delirium it was her worried face I saw. Sometimes I heard Rhiannon's voice or Simon's, but that was my fever talking. Dame Joan had sent them on ahead to Paris and then Rome. Once, as clear as day, I saw Will Belet sitting by my side.

"You can't be here," I said.

"Yes, I can, and I should be with you," he said.

"It isn't right." I was sore afraid.

"Very well," he answered, and vanished. But my fear remained.

Sir Raymond and Peter stayed to wait on the outcome of my illness. Dame Joan has told me many times since that she was certain I'd die in St. Denis, and that her task would be to return my body to England.

I didn't die. I felt death calling me. I felt how easy it would be to surrender to it, yet something held me to life. I came out of the fevers weak and pitiful as a near-drowned kitten, yet alive.

Dame Joan hired a litter to carry me to Paris. She kept the curtains drawn lest a malevolent breeze finish me off. I was glad to be hidden away from the eyes of the world, but sorry to see nothing of our approach to the city.

We stayed in rooms overlooking the Seine. The house was near the Petit Pont, the little bridge, where students of the city flocked to listen to famous teachers. Perhaps this was where Peter Abelard had once taught, where Heloise came to learn, and instead fell in love. It had ended so badly for both of them. Dame Joan had told me the story years ago as a cautionary tale against the dangers of love — or was it the dangers of learning?

I'd not ever wish to be Heloise, who lost her love and wound up in the convent, but I did envy the students I saw from my window. There they were rushing about or lounging on the stone benches of the bridge, in languid or heated debate. They seemed so free. I even saw a few girls with their chaperones. They might study, but they weren't free. Mostly the students were clerics who'd left their villages and towns. Some had left their countries for Paris.

"Fie on the students," fumed Dame Joan, "arguing all the day and carousing all the night."

There had been quite a few drunken brawls under our windows. I didn't mind. I was still too close to death to mind any of the little disturbances of life. But I did mind the spectre of Sir Runcival. I realized that he could come to Paris just as easily as I.

"We must leave here," I begged. "We are too close to England. He'll find me. He'll take me back. Please, we must go at once to Rome."

"My child," soothed Dame Joan. "How you talk! You are safe. Sir Raymond is here to protect you, and so am I."

"We must get to Rome."

At least Sir Runcival was a fear I could name. I still had the feeling, more persistent than ever, that I was suffocating. And now I was troubled by fleeting spirits. I'd hear a faint cry, behind me, like the mewling of a kitten. When I twisted around to see what was there, I'd find nothing at all. Nothing at all.

"What is it?" asked Dame Joan. "You look as if you've seen a ghost."

"No, it is nothing. I merely startled myself."

"Perhaps it is something," said Dame Joan. "Something you don't wish to see."

"It's Sir Runcival," I said. "He's after me and we must flee."

Dame Joan crossed herself. "I don't think that is what's troubling you. Drink this good broth," she said. "Eat your meat. We cannot leave until you are stronger."

I knew she was right. I knew I was too weak to

travel. But I didn't care if I died on my way to Rome. That didn't worry me nearly as much as the thought of Sir Runcival, or the cry that had no form, or the weight on my chest. I realized that my fears were too great, that they might be part of my sickness; yet I was caught in them.

At night I dreamed of trying to escape from a fog-shrouded *thing*. My heart pounded. I could not breathe. My legs could not run fast enough. It was ever just behind me. What was it that made me so fearful? I looked over my shoulder and saw Will Belet. Now my heart beat with joy; I gulped great draughts of air, cold and pure. As I reached out to take his hand, I heard the kitten's cry. That was my duty! I had to find the kitten. It was wrong to be with Will. I turned and ran right into the arms of Sir Runcival.

I woke screaming and bathed in sweat.

"Lady Edith, Lady Edith." Dame Joan wept and rocked me. "What demon has you in its grasp?"

"Please take me to Rome."

"I can fight any illness," said Dame Joan. "But I am no match for the evil that harries you. I fear you are possessed. Perhaps our only hope is to get to His Holiness."

Was I possessed? No. At least, I didn't think so.

"My fears are real enough," I said.

"It's that Welsh witch. She's cast a spell on you," said Dame Joan. "I knew she was a demon the moment I set eyes on her."

"No!" I said. "Rhiannon is only a girl. There's no harm in her."

"Hmph!"

"I think she was sent to help me."

"Did Satan help Eve?"

I didn't tell Dame Joan how Rhiannon was able to read my heart and thoughts. To Dame Joan that would be clear proof of sorcery. I needed Rhiannon to help me sort out my dreams and fears. I needed her to see what I could not — the mysteries of my own heart. I missed her, and Simon. I missed their laughter most of all. If Simon and Rhiannon were here they could have explored Paris for me. Even if I wasn't well enough to go out, they would have brought Paris to me with the tales of what they'd seen.

By the time we'd been in Paris a fortnight, my terrors had grown so intense that Dame Joan was looking as hollow-eyed as I. If I could have suffered in silence, and spared her, I would have. But my cries came from the depth of my sleep, and I had no control over them. One afternoon she announced that we would leave the very next day for Rome.

"Lord knows, the going may kill you," she said, "but the staying will surely kill us both."

I kissed her and wept. She hugged me and cried, too. That night was the first since leaving England that I slept through, without any dreams at all.

The sun smiled the morning we left Paris. The air smelled softly of spring. I insisted on riding my mare, though I wasn't sure I'd be able to keep my seat.

"I cannot be carried all the way to Rome," I said.

I could tell Dame Joan wanted to argue, but couldn't. It would be impossible to carry me to Rome.

"We shall go slowly," she said. "And you must promise to let me know when you are tired."

"I promise."

"You must say something *before* you collapse."

"I understand."

"With your leave, milady?" Sir Raymond stepped forward to lift me onto my horse. It was the first I'd seen of him since he'd carried me from the litter to my bed in Paris.

"Good, Sir Raymond," I said. "I'd be grateful."

He scooped me up in his brawny arms.

"Ah, mistress, will you not let Dame Joan fatten you up?" he said. "You're as weightless as my peregrine."

"But, Sir Raymond," I said, "I am meant to be a peregrine."

He looked puzzled. No doubt Dame Joan had told him I was bewitched. He probably thought I considered myself a falcon.

"Peregrine is another word for pilgrim," I said.

"Aye," he said, and managed a smile. "I'd forgotten the word has that meaning, too."

I liked Sir Raymond's idea. I'd rather be his sort of peregrine, soaring high above my troubles. It would be better by far than plodding along, bound to the earth.

Peter walked by my side. I imagined Dame Joan had set him the task of catching me should I tumble from my mare. I was glad of his company. The streets were so crowded we had to ride single file. Sir Raymond led the way, his massive charger parting the throng. I followed him, Dame Joan rode behind me, and three yeomen guarded our rear and the two packhorses.

Paris was the grandest place I'd ever been. Each street we came to held some new marvel. Narrow wooden and stone houses stood snug, side by side. Shops on the ground floor displayed brilliant banners or painted wooden signs showing the goods or services found within. Spice shops! Furriers! Goldsmiths! Bootmakers! Money changers!

Maids and youths walked about with trays of delicious-looking pasties. Men and women sold vegetables, candles, and live chickens. There were seamstresses with scissors, needle, and thread.

"Mend your cloak! Stitch a sleeve!" they cried.

One man carried wine in a copper bowl which he banged with a dipper. "Sample today's wine," he called. "The best Burgundy to be had in all of Paris. Drink it at Henri's on the Rue de Lapin."

Elegant ladies and knights walked about in the

finest silvery furs. Brooches crusted with fat jewels, bracelets, and rings fit for kings were worn quite casually.

"Is it a fair this day?" I asked Peter.

"Nay," he said. " 'Tis like this every day in Paris."

This was the adventure I'd hoped to have when I left England. And here I was running away from it. Perhaps I *was* possessed.

VIII. Queen Eleanor and Dame Margery

We passed through the market of Rue de Garlande. All the bustle and life I'd seen in the crowded streets was here a hundred times over. Farmers sold leafy greens, spring onions, butter, and rounds of cheese from their carts. Chickens, ducks, and geese complained loudly in their wicker baskets. Away from the farmers, bejeweled gloves, glowing carpets, spices, and perfumes were displayed by richly dressed merchants.

On a small raised platform a juggler spun balls in the air. Nearby a sad-looking bear did a lumbering dance when his master tugged his chain.

"Poor bear," I said.

"Mistress," said Peter, "'tis only a bear."

"Aye."

"Make way! Make way!" A herald boomed and a small procession forced its way into the square.

"His Royal Highness, Louis the Seventh, King of

France. Her Royal Highness, Eleanor of Aquitaine, Queen of France." The herald continued to shout above the increasing uproar in the market, as the lowly and the highborn tried to make way.

Sir Raymond moved protectively in front of me, so at first I couldn't see Their Majesties. I edged my mare to the side and came nearly face to face with the queen. There was no mistaking her. This was the woman Rhiannon wanted to meet — the bringer of light. She was beautiful, proud, elegant — the most regal person I'd ever seen. Beside her rode the pale young king, looking more like a virtuous cleric than the crowned head of France.

The queen looked my way and smiled warmly.

"Ah peregrine!" she said, no doubt seeing the cross on my cloak. "Whither do you go?" Her voice was lilting, like a song.

I bowed.

"Your Majesty, we are bound for Rome, on our way to Jerusalem."

Her eyes lit up.

"Happy pilgrim! Would that I could join you." Then her eyes went dull and blank; her smile waned. "But I cannot."

Unable to think of any words to say, I bowed again. When I looked up, she had moved on. The crowd closed in around the royal couple, and I could see her no more.

"Such an honor, Lady Edith," said Dame Joan,

pinkly glowing. "That Her Majesty should speak to you directly!"

I nodded, barely hearing her.

Sir Raymond turned in his saddle, and seemed to regard me with new respect.

"May we continue on our way?" I asked.

"Indeed, milady, as you wish," he said. And soon he'd cleared a path for our exit from the square.

"The queen spoke to *my* lady," said Peter. "Oh, mistress, I'm so proud!"

I suppose it was exciting to speak with the queen. But I was too amazed by her words and the sad look in her eyes to pay much attention to anything else. She'd called me "happy pilgrim." She wanted to go with me, and could not. She was as trapped with King Louis, as I would be with Sir Runcival. Not even being heiress of Aquitaine and Queen of France could open her cage. Rhiannon had said Queen Eleanor had brought the sun of Provence to the gloomy old Louvre. It looked more as if the Louvre had eclipsed the queen's sun.

"What a fine looking woman is the queen," said Dame Joan. "I can't say the same for His Majesty. Pity!"

"Aye." The beautiful, sad queen envied me. It made me sadder still, and eager to put Paris behind me. I held tightly to the reins and concentrated on Sir Raymond's broad back.

Before long we were on the road heading away from

Paris, and eventually leading to Rome. Dame Joan came up beside me now that the road was wider.

"Are you all right, Lady Edith?"

I forced a smile and tried to sit straighter on my horse.

The Rue de Garlande took us past an enormous ancient building of great blocks of stone and huge marble columns. Some of the walls were crumbling, and the roof was only partly intact.

"What is this place?" I asked.

Dame Joan crossed herself. "It's the devil's work," she said. "Only demons could build such a monstrosity."

Sir Raymond turned in his saddle to face us.

"It's called the Palais de Hautefeuille," he said.

"The Palace of Lofty Leaves," I said. "What does that mean?"

Sir Raymond shrugged. "I don't know. Some say it was built by Saracens. More likely it is left from the Roman times."

"Pagans!" said Dame Joan and crossed herself again. "Giant pagan demons!"

Perhaps the Romans had been giants to build such huge palaces. I hadn't given much thought to what lay ahead, I'd been so concerned with getting away from what lay behind me. Now I began to wonder about Rome. How much of the pagan city was left? How would it be to walk and talk and eat in the midst of such enormities? I could well imagine Simon and Rhiannon being perfectly content in the land of pagan giants, but how would I feel?

What of the Holy Father's realm? Simon would be sure to find a welcome there. Would I? Could I find peace and safety? At least, in the Holy City the laws of the church would be honored. I'd not be forced into a marriage I abhorred. In England or France Sir Runcival might be able to find a priest to do his bidding. In the shadow of the Holy See no cleric would so desecrate his robes. Perhaps the pope would give me his blessing and some sort of document, a papal bull, to guarantee my freedom.

It was a possibility. It was something to hope for, and I'd had so little hope. Yet Rome was a long way off. I sighed.

"You are tired," said Dame Joan. "We'll stop and rest."

"Nay. We've only just begun," I said. "We'll keep going."

The road took us through fields and villages. Occasionally I saw the forbidding tower of a castle rising high above its walls on a distant hill. I began to see that this was, indeed, a different land. These were not the fields, nor the hills of England. This was France, and I was glad.

We were headed for Vezelay. It was a few days' ride south of Paris. The sun was smiling on us and the air was soft. Wild hyacinths and yellow cuckoo flowers bloomed along the road.

"It is spring," I said, amazed by its suddenness.

"Yes," said Dame Joan. "Before long it will be summer."

We could see the spire of La Madeleine, the church of Mary Magdalene, from miles away. The grandest church in Burgundy, perhaps in all of France, was set at the summit of the hill town of Vezelay. All day we journeyed toward it, Dame Joan continually murmuring prayers to the Mother of God and the Reformed Sinner. Climbing the steep road up to the town, we lost sight of the church. Through the winding streets, ever upward we went.

"'Tis like climbing the road to heaven," said Dame Joan.

Eventually we came to the square and the great gray church looming above us.

"It is a miracle!" exclaimed Dame Joan.

I think she meant the huge church in front of us.

We left the horses to be cared for by the yeomen and walked into the yawning door. Dame Joan was leaning heavily on my arm, her face radiant and fearful. I was doing my best to support her, and not stumble. The church was magnificent, awesome. The nave, a parade of warmly glowing limestone, led to the pure white altar of pointed arches soaring up to impossible heights. Dame Joan was weeping. Peter and Sir Raymond also seemed deeply moved. I could see that it was thrilling. But its grandeur did not move me. Furthermore, I was puzzled. Why was La Madeleine a "miracle," and the Palais de Hautefeuille the work of demons?

"Let us pay homage to the sainted Magdalene," said Dame Joan. We followed the winding stone steps down to the old crypt, below the altar.

Dame Joan passionately kissed the saint's reliquary. I kissed it, too, but with little feeling. I saw the beauty, and the holiness, but my heart did not respond. The crypt was too much like the dark chapel where Bertrade de Montfort and King Philip were buried. I didn't want to be reminded of them. Will Belet had crept into my dreams, but I tried not to think of him when I was awake. When I was married it would have been wrong to think of him. Perhaps now it wasn't. I didn't know, and there was no one I could ask. What would be the point to think of Will Belet? He wasn't my Philip; he was my friend.

Had Rhiannon been standing near, and heard that thought, she'd surely have pinched me. All right, Will Belet was more than a friend. And I had loved him. But what did it matter? Will might be anywhere in England or Anjou, serving Lord Henry. He'd be living a great adventure. He'd have no reason to remember me.

And yet Simon said Will did remember me — "in his every letter." I hoped that he remembered the bold, free girl I'd been. When Will and I were together I was so filled with joy, I felt I could fly.

That was then. He was a penniless second son, and I. . . . There had been nothing between us and no chance of there ever being anything. Our lives were set on different courses. Our story ended when I married Sir Bohemund. There was no reason at all to think of him.

"Are you tired?" asked Dame Joan.

"Yes," I said. I was tired of the noise inside my head and of this dark and holy place.

Sir Raymond swept me into his arms and carried me up from the crypt to the blazing, bright church. And out we went to the softer light of day, to the terrace overlooking the Yonne River and the green and flowering valley. While Peter went to get us something to eat, Dame Joan arranged a carpet and pillows for us to sit on.

"I hope it won't be too damp," she fussed. "No sense taking a chill. Yet it is a sweet day, and the sun may put some roses on your cheeks."

She bustled about, talking partly to me, mostly to herself. For all her energy, Dame Joan looked more worn than ever I'd seen her. Poor Old Wobbly Chins. She'd had a burdensome time with me. In the future, I'd try not to worry her so.

From Vezelay we continued south. The road was wearying, but the farther we went, the better I felt. We stayed in the austere guest houses of abbeys, and in filthy inns. Once we stayed in a stable, and picked hay from our clothes all the next day. On several clear nights we slept under the stars. I liked that best of all, but it was very hard on Sir Raymond, who stood guard, and Dame Joan, who was terrified of wandering spirits and brigands. Sir Raymond had a friend near the town of Macon. We stayed for several days in his large and well-situated manor overlooking the Saone River.

At night I lulled myself to sleep repeating the names of the new places I'd seen and the ones still to come. *Godstone, Dover, Boulogne, St. Denis.* . . . It became a charm against worries. . . . *Paris, Vezelay, Lyons, Provence, Marseilles, Rome.* . . . It didn't stop my dreams, but, when I woke fearful in the night, I'd say the place names until my heart stopped racing and I could slip back into sleep.

The road seemed to fill up with travelers. There were many merchants: dark-eyed, dusky Italians, round and red-nosed Dutch from the Low countries, and pale, tall Norsemen. I was most curious about the small band of Saracen merchants we saw heading north to Paris. But Dame Joan wouldn't even let me look on them too closely. And she shivered when they passed.

Clerics traveled on church business. Liveried squires carried news. Armored knights rode off to war, or as escorts to fine ladies and little children. There were pilgrims come from all over, men and women from as far away as Ireland. Mostly they were heading for Rome. A few said they were also bound for the Holy Land. It seemed that the whole world was going, or coming. I'd been longing my entire life for this, dreaming of traveling. Finally I was part of the restless movement, part of the greater world. We stayed one night at the Abbey of St. Aubin with a group of pilgrims from England, also bound for Jerusalem. In their midst was a most determinedly holy woman, Margery Kempe. She was given to visions, sighing, shouting, crying, and, most irksome of all, instruction.

Throughout our supper at the prior's table she lamented without ceasing.

"I see the white light of the beautiful Saint Brigitte," she exclaimed, "its blessed beauty leading us to the path of righteousness." Then she sighed deeply. "If only the doubters had faith." She looked round the table, reprovingly.

"Please, Dame Margery," said the priest in their company. "We are trying to sup in tranquility."

"Aye," wailed Margery. "There can be no tranquility, but in the Lord's grace." And she skewered me with her gaze.

She was a mad busybody. Normally, I'd not pay her the slightest heed. But she was right. I was not tranquil, and I didn't feel in His grace. I turned my head to avoid her look.

"Visions of saints whilst honest people are at their meat," muttered Dame Joan. Dame Margery had been preaching at us since the moment our paths had crossed early in the morning. Dame Joan had had quite an earful of admonition and advice. "I pray our path and Dame Margery's will soon part."

I prayed that, too. Yet, in spite of her laments and exhortations, there was something appealing about Margery Kempe. She was so sure of herself, and her divine visions — so much surer than I. She was following the straight and true road to her soul's salvation in Jerusalem. My feet walked along that same road, but my heart and soul were lost on a different twisted path of mad dreams and fears. I knew not where that path led. How simple it would be to be Margery Kempe, secure in the Lord's grace, plowing ever forward without doubts or fears.

I conjured a vision of Dame Margery dispatching Sir Runcival with the weight and persistence of her holy wrath. It was a wonderful thought.

"What is the matter?" asked Dame Joan. "You're smiling."

"Have I smiled so little of late that it is cause for concern?"

"Aye," said Dame Joan.

"I merely thought of something funny," I said.

"Oh," she said, but continued to eye me warily.

IX.
The Three Tibors

Dame Joan became uneasy as soon as we crossed into the hilly region of Provence.

"I don't like it," she said. "The people are too dark and shifty-looking. The land is harsh, and the sun too strong. 'Tis a worrisome place."

Her fears were justified. Outside of Lyons we met a ragged band of men armed with staves and knives. Sir Raymond seemed to expand to twice his normal girth.

"Make way!" he growled. "Let the Holy Pilgrims pass in peace, or suffer my wrath."

Sir Raymond unsheathed his sword, and the men edged off the road, but eyed us evilly as we passed. Sir Raymond proceeded calmly, but hastened us to the safety of Lyons' walls.

"If not for our good knight," said Dame Joan, "those varlets would have done us ill."

She was right. Had Sir Raymond been a lesser man, they would have attacked. I didn't admit as much to Dame Joan. But I, too, was unnerved by the "varlets."

"I can't make head nor tails of what these Provençals are saying," Dame Joan complained the next day.

The *Langue d'Oc* was the language of the south. It was quite different from the northern French that we knew. Had she imagined all men from England to Jerusalem would speak her tongue? I loved the strange new language. When I concentrated and the Provençals spoke slowly enough, I began to understand it. But more than the *Langue d'Oc* I loved the sky, so azure blue it hurt my eyes, the heat, the pungent taste of garlic and olives, and the swarthy, raven-haired southerners.

"Don't you think I could pass for a Provençal?" I asked Dame Joan.

"Never!" She seemed horrified. "How can you say such a thing?"

My fearless old nurse, for once, was daunted.

Sir Raymond came from Poitiers and had many friends in Provence. We climbed one of the numerous cragged hills, webbed with grapevines, to stay at Sarenom, castle of Guilhem d'Omelas and his darkly handsome wife, Tibors d'Orange.

The Lady Tibors had two daughters, each named Tibors as was the custom in those parts.

"It's absolutely absurd!" said Dame Joan. "Three women with the same name under one roof, and all of them as alike as peas in a pod."

"The older daughter is called Tiborine," I said. "And the younger one is Tiburgette. It's simple enough."

"It's all nonsense, the names and the 'poesifying.' It's not proper for ladies. I wish we were beyond France and in the pope's care."

I was always the one wanting to push forward, but I was content to stay with the three Tibors until Sir Raymond deemed the horses well rested. I suspected he needed respite from the constant company of Dame Joan and me more than the horses needed rest. Guilhem d'Omelas and Sir Raymond had shared many a battle. The men sat in the great hall, reliving those memories. Though each story ended with some noble comrade's death, they seemed happy remembering.

I was fascinated by the "poesifying," as Dame Joan called it. Tibors, her daughters, and the ladies of her court were caught up in a game I'd never heard of before.

"That's because England is too uncivilized for courtly love," Tiborine said, teasing me.

The ladies' days were spent in their room, the sun-drenched solar, or the lush gardens. The southern sun penetrated the very marrow of my bones. For the first time in my life I knew what it meant to be truly warm. I couldn't get enough of the sun, and the strongly scented garden.

"We have rosemary and thyme in England," said Dame Joan.

"But not like this," I said. The paths were planted with herbs so that every footstep released aromatic clouds.

"Come out of the sun," said Dame Joan.

Never.

"Your nose is turning bright pink."

Reluctantly I obeyed.

We only joined the men in the hall for the heavy midday meal. Some of the women worked embroidery, or wove fine linen, but most of the ladies wielded pen or lute. They made up songs as did the jongleurs of England, although they didn't sing of war and knightly feats. Instead, they sang of men and women — of love.

"It's sinful," cried Dame Joan when one of Tibors's verses was translated for her.

"Sweet, beloved one," sang Tibors, plucking the strings of her lute.

It was sinful because the song was about a married woman and her lover. Yet I knew Lady Tibors loved Sir Guilhem. I saw it in their laughter and easy embraces. They were very like my own loving mother and father. Nearly all the songs told a similar story. Even Tiborine, who still wore deep mourning for her young husband, sang songs of love and lovers. I'd never breathe such words. But for the three Tibors it was some sort of game. And though it was a game, it was played in earnest. The women argued over the shades of meaning in their verses. They sought the *rima cara*, the dear rhyme, in which a word was rhymed with itself. Sometimes they wrote songs about the friendship of women. Sometimes they sang of children and childhood. Each verse and the tune that accompanied it underwent many revisions. It was as painstaking as the finest embroidery, yet capturing the right word was as thrilling as a hunt for boar.

I tried to ignore what made me blush and concentrate on the *trobairitz*, as they called themselves. These women were doing something I'd never considered. They wrote beautiful songs about the worlds that women ruled. Although they remained within the castle's walls their words made them free.

"Sweet, beloved one . . ."

I pondered the song I might write. I wouldn't write about love; my song would be about the peregrine, flying high in an azure sky.

"Sweet, beloved one . . . an hour does not pass that I do not think of you. Would that you, too, had a thought for me."

I thought of Will Belet. I didn't want to, but Lady Tibors's song conjured him, and I found it impossible to dismiss him. The more I thought about him, the more I enjoyed remembering our times together. I wondered if Will still had Uther, the fine hunting dog that Father had given him. How we had laughed at Uther, the puppy. How sweet Will was with that dog. Though I tried to shut him out, Will was ever in my thoughts, especially now.

My days at Sarenom were spent entranced by the three Tibors and the other ladies. I studied their lovely silken dresses, of so many bright colors, like a summer garden. Some of the women wore wimples, but often their hair was loose, or plaited and piled in swirls on their heads. As they wove their songs, their dark eyes flashed. Sometimes the music would swell beyond the confines of a song. Then Tiburgette would leap to her feet, and pull her sister into a whirling skipping dance. All but the oldest ladies joined in. I danced with them until my legs gave out. Dame Joan didn't even scold me. She saw my health and strength beginning to return in the southern sun.

Dame Joan sat beside Dame Berengaria, one-time nurse of Tiborine and Tiburgette. The two of them condemned the "poesifying" as they mended our travel-worn gowns and cloaks.

"Shameful!" said Dame Berengaria, and she'd translate the latest song for Dame Joan.

"Tsk, tsk! In front of the children," said Dame Joan.

"To think my own sweet nurslings are saying these dreadful things." Dame Berengaria crossed herself. "They certainly didn't learn any of these tricks from me!" Then she glared at Lady Tibors. The lady laughed, and gave the old nurse a kiss before taking up her lute again.

"Lady Edith," coaxed Tiburgette, "won't you write a song for us of English love?"

"No, I couldn't," I said and felt my face reddening yet again.

"Do not impose upon our guest," said Lady Tibors.

"Please, Maman, mayn't I ask Lady Edith for her story that we may learn about the faraway England?"

"Only if Lady Edith agrees."

"There's not much to tell," I said. "My husband died and left me a wealthy widow."

"How kind of him!" said Tiburgette.

"He was kind," I said.

"How sad you have lost him," said Tiborine.

And my babe, but I wouldn't speak of that. If Rhiannon had been by my side she'd have pinched me hard for all that I didn't mention.

"But why do you wander so far from home?" asked Tiborine.

"There was nothing to hold me to my home." Again I could feel what would have been Rhiannon's impatience with me. "And had I stayed, King Stephen would have married me off to an evil man."

"Stay here with us!" cried Tiburgette. "You are happy here, yes?"

"Yes, but my road continues. My brother and my friend await me in Rome," I said. "I hope that the pope can help me. Then I'll continue on to Jerusalem."

"The Lord will protect and guide you," said Lady Tibors. "And may He bring you back to us."

"I hope it will be so," I said. "I'll bring my friend, Rhiannon. You will like her."

"Rhiannon," said Tiborine. "A Welsh name, isn't it?"

"Yes," I said.

"The Countess of Bordeaux is Welsh," said Tiburgette.

"A most admired lady," said Tiborine; she turned to her mother. "Didn't she have a Welsh princess in her care?"

I wondered if the Countess of Bordeaux was connected to Rhiannon. She had said that the French queen would have been interested in her family. Perhaps the countess was whom she meant. Could the ragtag girl I'd found in the king's forest be kin to a French countess?

At night, I breathed without choking. I listened as the intoxicating songs swam through my mind. My own song began to take shape:

High flying wanderer,
freely come, and freely go.

Will Belet drifted in and out of my thoughts. I wondered what he was doing now. Perhaps Simon knew, and I could ask him when I got to Rome. I prayed Will was safe. Sir Runcival continued to haunt my dreams, but even his evil aspect was not so threatening here.

No, I would not write of love. But the song of the peregrine increasingly filled my thoughts.

I twisted words around as I lay abed next to Dame Joan. The surrounding darkness and her soft snoring helped set my mind free. I thought of my own flight from Sir Runcival. I thought of the look I'd seen in Queen Eleanor's eyes. She, too, would have flown if she could. I saw again Rhiannon's face as I'd first seen it, wild and begrimed. She was also a bird in flight.

Fly above the mountains,
under the golden sun.
Fly, peregrine, beyond
the grasping one.

It wasn't very good, but it was mine. During the five days left of our stay, I constantly juggled the words to catch my meaning, and to understand what I meant to say.

On the eve of our departure I gathered my courage and ventured to speak privately with my hostess.

"Milady Tibors, I . . ." I began and faltered.

"Yes, Lady Edith, you?"

"I've composed a song for you," I mumbled.

"How charming!" she said. "Ladies! Our guest has a gift for us. Please be still and listen."

Dame Joan looked stricken. I'm sure she was afraid I'd spout love poetry, and shame her before Dame Berengaria.

"It isn't a love poem," I said quickly, before Dame Joan hushed me. "I've written it in my words, and trust that Tiborine will translate for me."

The solar was quiet, waiting. This was a new kind of fear to stand before them, and I was sorry I'd begun. Yet I had to finish. Tiborine nodded and smiled encouragement.

"Peregrine," I said and cleared my throat. I sang without a lute, and I know my voice wavered.

Fly swiftly high,
pierce the azure sky.
Freely come, and
freely go.

Fly above the mountains,
under the golden sun.
Fly, peregrine, beyond
the grasping one.

Falcon wandering
from land to land,
wondering, is it ever
safe to land?

Fly swiftly high,
pierce the azure sky.
Freely come, and
freely go.

X.
Mirabilia Urbis Romae

As soon as we arrived in Rome, we sent Peter to the Lateran Palace to find Simon. He and Brothers Eustace, John, and Aldobert were guests at the cloister attached to the palace. I wasn't sure where Rhiannon was, but Simon would know.

We were staying in rooms quite near the Lateran. The house was almost as pleasant as the castle of the three Tibors. Our windows faced away from the palace toward the green Alban hills and the cool breezes of the Mediterranean. The house had three stories. On the street level was a shop selling wine, olives, and olive oil. It was run by the stout mistress of the house, the Signora. She lived in a room behind the shop with several noisy, curly-haired children. Above us, in the garret, were quiet-as-mice German clerks who had business at the Lateran Palace. We had the whole first floor. "The *piano nobile!*" said the Signora. "The best for the Noble Lady."

The Signora had insisted on showing us every inch of it, no matter how I protested our fatigue. Our rooms all had slippery floors of highly polished stone, made from various colored marble.

"*Terrazzo!*" said the Signora. She made me touch its icy surface, perhaps so I'd understand how cool and comfortable our rooms would be.

At tedious length, the Signora explained how to open and close the sliding shutters to keep out the midday sun and rain. I pretended to listen, occasionally nodding my head when it seemed required. The Signora spoke a smattering of French and English, which she mixed freely with her native Italian. Surprisingly, I understood her very well. But I was deadly tired. I wanted to see Simon and Rhiannon, and that was all I could think about.

"Thank you. Thank you," I said, ushering the Signora out the door.

"*Grazie*, to you, Lady *Donna*," she said.

"And *grazie*, to you," I said, shutting the door firmly.

Dame Joan had ignored the Signora completely, devoting herself to unpacking our chest, and clucking over our shabby clothes.

I hoped to sojourn at least a month in Rome, perhaps two. Dame Joan and I needed to rest and grow stronger before we attempted the final leg of our journey. Even more, I looked forward to spending the time with Rhiannon and Simon. When we'd leave for the Holy Land, Simon would remain for a while in Rome before returning to Godstone. This was my chance to be with my brother before life parted us again. What could be better, than to be together in Rome? Just on our entry into the city, I'd seen such sights: a huge column covered with carvings, a giant archway, a pyramid, strange round and oval-shaped buildings. All of it was so enormous; the ancient Romans must have been giants indeed. I wanted to explore it all with Simon and Rhiannon — *after* I was rested. Poor Dame Joan and I were bone weary.

"Edith!" exclaimed Simon, bursting into the solar. "How thin and wan you look! But we'll fatten you up, and the Roman sun will give you some color."

Such an imp! What a way to greet me. Naturally, he'd forgotten that I'd been ill. Well, I'd not remind him. I was so happy to see him, and glad that he didn't bring up my illness. I'd just as soon have it forgotten.

"You know that ladies take great pains to avoid the sun," I said.

"That's absurd!" he cried. "Surely you don't think a deathly pallor becomes you."

"I suppose, if I look deathly . . ."

"Well, that's enough about your complexion," said Simon. "I can't wait to show you Rome. Let's start with the Capitol."

"Simon, have mercy. I've been traveling without a day's repose since we left Provence."

"All right, then we'll start with the Palace. Though I don't suppose there's time to arrange for an audience with His Holiness."

"Nonsense!" said Dame Joan. "Can't you see your sister is nearly done in from traveling?" Dame Joan let fall the robe she'd been shaking out, and sank onto the chest. She sighed. "And I am, too."

"Forgive me," said Simon, dropping to his knees before her. "I'm so happy you're both here. The whole world is to be seen in Rome, and I want to show you every wondrous bit of it."

"Soon enough, child." She took his chin in her hand to study him more closely. "I'm glad being out in the world has not changed you."

She was right. Simon was still Simon, and still more child than man.

"Where is Rhiannon?" I asked.

"I'm afraid she's been this whole time locked up with the Sisters of St. Cecilia, and not very happy about it."

"How awful for her!" Why hadn't I thought of that, that they would shut her up in a convent? Not that there were any other options. "You must have her sent here, immediately," I said.

"I've written a letter to the abbess in your hand," said Simon. "All it wants is your signature and seal."

"I'm surprised you didn't sign and seal it yourself," I said as Simon produced a horn of ink and a sharpened quill.

"I thought of it," said Simon. "But had I gotten her out, I couldn't think where to put her."

"While you're gone, Lady Edith and I will rest," said Dame Joan.

I helped her labor to her feet and into our bedchamber. She dropped onto the bed and sighed deeply. She'd be asleep within moments. I was as tired as Dame Joan, but I wanted to be alone with Simon.

"Shall I go now to release Rhiannon?" he asked when I returned to the antechamber.

"Not just yet," I said. "It's been so long since I've seen you. Tell me more of you, of Rome."

"Well, I've been at work in the Scriptorium of the Lateran. It is an inspiration simply to sit there."

As I listened to Simon, I was aware of the soft snoring of Dame Joan, falling into deep sleep. This was my chance.

"Have you heard from Will Belet?" I asked. It came out before I'd been able to cloak it in indifference. Simon seemed nearly as startled as I.

"What?" he said.

"I know you heard me."

"Yes. Yes, we've exchanged letters since I've been in Rome."

"How does he?"

"He is well," said Simon.

"And?" Was Simon teasing me, or being terribly obtuse?

"And what, Lady Edith?"

He *was* teasing.

"What do his letters *say*, Brother Simon?"

"They speak of you."

"Truly?"

Simon nodded. "I wrote him that you were ill, and he's been concerned."

"Thank you." I breathed. "Now tell me something of him. Where is he? What does he do at the court of Lord Henry?"

"He is still in Anjou, but there is talk of going to England to join the Empress Matilda. Much of his day is spent in study with the young lord."

"Like clerks?"

"They are becoming as learned as clerks," said Simon. "And Lord Henry has a particular interest in law. He reads that while Will pursues his studies in the healing arts. Will Belet is becoming a fine physician."

I don't know what I'd imagined, perhaps that Will spent all his days in the tilting yard, jousting, or in mock combat. But I liked thinking of Will as a scholar. Learning to read at Woburn Abbey was the one thing that made being there bearable. Perhaps I should read something now besides my prayer book. With Simon's help, I could become a scholar, too.

Simon was grinning at me. "Lady Edith, does my news please you?"

"Yes," I said. "It does." I felt my face coloring. "Now, please, go to Rhiannon."

"At once," said Simon. He turned to leave, but stopped at the door. "I'm glad you're better, Edith."

"Thank you, Simon."

When he was gone, I crawled into bed beside Dame Joan. I closed my weary eyes. New — and intriguing — images of Will Belet filled my head as I fell into sleep.

Rhiannon did not say one word to me for an entire week. She was always at my side, but her displeasure with me showed in her every look and gesture. At first I tried coaxing her with gentle entreaties. I begged her pardon repeatedly for not having kept her with me, although, at the time, I was too ill to have protested Dame Joan's decision. I didn't put the blame on Dame Joan for sending Rhiannon away; there was already too much enmity between them. Soon I gave it all up. Rhiannon always knew my mind; I had no need to speak it. There was no use coaxing or teasing her into speech. Only when she was ready would Rhiannon talk to me.

We spent our first week in Rome visiting with Simon and Brother Eustace, when the cloister could spare them, sleeping away long stretches of the day, and eating delicious food.

Dame Joan was always suspicious of the Signora's cooking, but Rhiannon, Sir Raymond, and I ate great quantities of all the food served. And I drank deeply of the dark red wine from the Alban hills.

"Have you forgotten all your manners, Lady Edith?" Dame Joan nettled. "You're as greedy and graceless as a villein."

She was right. Yet I couldn't stop myself; I was eating to fill up the deep pit within me.

After the midday meal, Rhiannon, Dame Joan, and I retired to the bedchamber. The Signora assured us that all of Rome observed this custom. I'd fall onto the soft, wide bed and into the heaviest sleep I'd ever known. I was still troubled by dreams of the crying kitten that would not be found, and the evil Sir Runcival. Other times I dreamed of Will Belet and no longer found those dreams so disturbing. The good food and the deep sleep were only part of my contentment. I had a secret hope, that Pope Lucius would be my protector. What's more, I had a plan.

At the end of our first week in Rome, when Dame Joan and I were rested enough to tour the city, Simon took us up to the once famous Roman capitol.

We climbed a steep path to get to a rough pasture littered with great blocks of stone, broken columns, and fragmented statues. To our right was a new building, and to our left, an abbey.

"This was once the head of the world," said Simon, showing us the barren hill where a few goats searched for grass. "Roman senators and consuls governed the earth from here."

"I've seen better hills in Oxfordshire," Dame Joan said with a sniff.

"You have to imagine the grandeur of it," said Simon. He raised his arms to paint a picture in the air. "Right here was a vast fortress, covered over with glass and gold. There were images of all the Trojan kings and the Roman emperors . . ."

I saw what Simon described and it raised prickles on my skin. To think that all that Roman greatness was now poor pasturage for a few goats.

". . . Inside was a palace, spectacular beyond belief, adorned with gold, silver, brass, and precious stones. And there were temples . . ."

"Let us go into yonder abbey church and pray," said Dame Joan.

She had to be desperate to sit down after the steep climb up the hill, and was certainly determined not to listen to lectures about pagans.

"Yes!" said Simon. "You must see the altar of the *Ara Coeli.*"

"Sounds pagan," said Dame Joan, looking doubtful.

"You'll see," said Simon, and he winked at me.

Rhiannon tugged on my hand. I could tell she was little inclined to enter the church. I imagined she'd had more than enough church since she'd been in Rome. We walked over to the edge of the hill and sat on a low wall.

"All that," said Rhiannon, pointing to the plain below us, "is the Roman Forum."

Her first words to me since St. Denis, and what she chose to discuss was this large field of ruins — of fallen blocks of marble and columns holding up the sky. Rhiannon would talk about pagan ruins, or nothing. So that's how it would be.

"How do you know what that is?" I asked. "Haven't you been captive all this time at the good sisters'?"

"You could care about the ancients, if only you'd let yourself. They have such wonderful stories to tell us. Look right here in front of you."

Would she ever answer a direct question?

"I am interested," I said. "I just wish you'd tell me . . ."

"Simon brought me here and to several other places in the city. He told the abbess I had business with the pope. And he gave me this book," she said, taking a slim volume from the pocket tied to her waist.

"*Mirabilia Urbis Romae,*" I read, and leafed through the book. It was a guide to the city, filled with stories about the ancient monuments. "The Marvels of Rome. I didn't know you could read."

Rhiannon gave me her most withering look.

"Are you ready to pay attention?"

"Yes."

"Can you see that bare spot over on the left?"

I nodded.

"That is Hell."

"What?"

"In the ancient times Hell burst forth from there."

"No!"

"Yes," she said, and I knew it was so.

I had the urge to cross myself, but resisted it. I was fascinated by the Romans, and frightened by what they'd been.

"What's that small round building?" I asked.

"The Temple of Vesta," she said. "It was tended by the Vestal Virgins. Next to the temple was their palace, one of the grandest in Rome. Their duty was to keep alive the sacred flame of Rome, and protect a statue of Pallas Athene, who was the guardian of the city."

"Were they nuns?" I asked.

"They were a noble and learned community of women," she said. "Although they took a vow of chastity, they were free to come and go as they pleased."

"Not like the nuns today."

"No," said Rhiannon.

"The Vestals remind me of the Tibors," I said, and for once, Rhiannon looked puzzled.

"They were three noblewomen I stayed with in Provence. They, and all of their companions, were dedicated to poetry and were . . ."

"The *trobairitz!*" exclaimed Rhiannon. "How lucky you are to have met them. I have heard of these enlightened Provençal women."

"And I believe that they have heard of *you*," I said.

"Oh?"

"They told me of a Welsh princess staying at the court of the Countess of Bordeaux."

"Imagine that," said Rhiannon, her eyes full of mischief. "A Welsh princess living with a French countess."

I couldn't tell if she was indeed that Welsh princess, or she thought it was nonsense. Before I could ask her, Dame Joan came storming out of the church.

"Your brother has been telling me the most ridiculous tale about a pagan emperor," she said.

"And the Sibyl's vision of the Virgin Mary?" asked Rhiannon, with just the faintest of smiles.

"I should have known!" cried Dame Joan, now angry in earnest. "You've put these notions into his head, pagan altars in a church. Ha! People burn for less. I'll not have you corrupting my Simon with your Welsh . . ."

"The story's from this book," said Rhiannon, holding up *Mirabilia Urbis Romae*, "that Simon gave me."

Dame Joan looked to me.

"Then it's probably true," I said.

"Yes," said Simon, joining us. "It's written by Benedict, a canon of St. Peter's. He knows all there is to know about Rome."

"Oh," said Dame Joan, looking defeated, and older than ever I'd seen her. This was not the Rome she'd been anticipating. The stories of pagan Rome were too alarming. Saints' miracles were one thing, but talk of sibyls and oracles was quite another.

We were to have our first audience with Pope

Lucius the following day. I had prepared a careful speech to ask His Holiness for protection from Sir Runcival. I hadn't told Simon or Dame Joan how I had my hopes set on the pontiff's help. If my plan failed, I didn't want them to know of my disappointment. Perhaps being in the presence of His Holiness, surrounded by all the other holy men, would reassure Dame Joan. Perhaps then she would feel better. I hoped I would, too.

XI. His Holiness, Pope Lucius

The morning of our audience with Pope Lucius, I tried to work out how best to present my petition to His Holiness. I hoped it wasn't wrong to ask for his help. I prayed he'd hear me.

First, I'd say that I was too grieved by the loss of my husband to remarry. . . . As soon as I had the thought, I wondered, Was it still true? Grief clung to me, but not for my dear husband.

Sir Bohemund had been sick for months. I'd had a long time to see his death coming. It made me sad, but I'd accepted it. In truth, it wasn't his death that kept me from remarrying. I didn't want Sir Runcival. I didn't want to be married off to a man that I loathed. Could I ask that of the pontiff? Could I beg him to protect me from an unwanted suitor?

What if he wouldn't listen? What if it was a mistake to ask? What hope would I have, then?

"Lady Edith! You've a rent in that gown." Dame Joan charged into the room. "Change it at once!"

"But the green gown is mud splattered, and there's that scorch mark on the damask rose," I said.

"Why can't you be more careful!" she scolded. "Haven't I told you often enough?"

Aye. She had.

"If you hadn't given away your best blue gown," she said, glaring at Rhiannon, who was wearing it, "you might be properly dressed now."

"I can wear the old gray gown, or the brown shroud the sisters gave me," said Rhiannon.

Was she trying to appease Dame Joan or exasperate her?

"Never!" said Dame Joan. "I'll not have one of the ladies in my care appear before the pontiff dressed as a convent servant!"

So Rhiannon had become a "lady" in Dame Joan's care. I wondered when that had happened. It seemed quite a leap from "that creature" and "the Welsh witch."

"Wear the damask, and cover the scorch mark with your embroidered pelisse," said Dame Joan, turning back to me.

"I cannot wear a fur-lined pelisse in June, in Rome," I said.

"At least you'll be presentable," said Dame Joan.

"I'll faint from the heat and embarrass us all," I said.

Dame Joan's lips were set in an angry line. "Very well! Stay in the mauve gown, though it doesn't suit you so well as the rose." Then she turned to Peter with fire in her eyes. "Bring me my sewing basket, and be quick about it."

Although we had passed by the Lateran Palace on our way to mass at the Basilica every day since our arrival in Rome, we had never ventured onto the portico. It was wide, deep, and tall, sheltering many ancient Roman statues. The rider of an equestrian statue greeted us with outstretched arm.

"Simon told me that this is a statue of Constantine the Great, the first Christian emperor," I said. "When the statue is once again covered in gold, as it was to begin with, it will signal the end of the world. A voice from the horse's forelock will announce the Last Judgment."

Dame Joan came forward and stroked the Emperor's foot. And then she saw the enormous head and hand that had been hidden in the shadows.

"Good Lord," she said. "What monster is this?"

I'd also been alarmed by the head when Simon had pointed it out to me on one of our morning rambles. Not only was it huge, but its eyes had a savage look.

"Simon told me it is the sun god who once stood in the huge oval temple some call the Colosseum. Pope Silvester destroyed the pagan temple and the rest of the statue."

"Why did he see fit to save the idol's head and

hand?" Dame Joan found it nearly impossible to walk past the monstrous head into the palace. "'Tis a demon wrought in stone," she said, crossing herself. "How can His Holiness allow such a thing?"

"It is only stone," said Rhiannon.

Did she really believe that, or was she merely trying to soothe Dame Joan? Her face gave nothing away. But Dame Joan seemed to heed her, at least enough to let us bring her into the palace.

Simon and Brothers Eustace, John, and Aldobert awaited us. Brother Eustace came quickly to assist Dame Joan.

"Madam, you seem discomfited," he said.

"It's that head out there," Dame Joan said and shivered.

"I, too, find it most disturbing," he said. That seemed to be the comfort she needed; she was soon restored to her usual self.

"Lady Edith, stand still and let me arrange your wimple. Rhiannon, leave your plaits bound. You may not appear before the pontiff with your hair loosed!"

Simon was nervous, as well — more than I'd ever seen him.

"What ails you?" I asked. "Are you frightened of His Holiness?"

"Frightened? No!" he said. Yet his face was ashen.

"What is it?" I persisted.

"Simon is showing the pope several pages of the

psalter he's been illuminating for His Holiness," said Rhiannon.

"Simon! The pope has charged you to work for him! Why haven't you told me?"

"Well . . ."

Simon was blushing. Blushing!

"What an honor for you, and how wonderful for Godstone!" I said.

Brother Eustace was beaming. "We've sent word to Abbot Bernard," he said. "It is the answer to our prayers."

"My little scamp," said Dame Joan, wiping away happy tears. "Who ever would have thought!"

"Beware the Sin of Pride," said Brother John, fastening Simon with a dour look.

"The canon beckons," said Brother Aldobert. "Let us proceed to His Holiness."

We followed the black-robed canon down a long corridor lined with colored marble and statues of naked and near naked men and women. Dame Joan clasped her hands in prayer, and kept her gaze downward.

"So why are you so nervous?" I spoke in Simon's ear.

"His Holiness liked the first book I gave him, but these paintings are different, of subjects the pontiff selected. What if he doesn't like how I've painted them?"

"Are you truly afraid of that?"

He nodded.

I doubted whether Dame Joan or Brother Aldobert would approve, but I took hold of my little brother's sweaty hand. "You've *nothing* to fear," I said, and kissed him.

His eyes searched mine. "Thank you, Edith."

With his hand in mine, we entered the presence of the holiest man in Christendom.

We approached the papal throne at the far end of the large hall. On the walls and ceiling were mosaics in jewel colors of apostles and saints surrounded by fields of blooming flowers. Centered over the throne, the ceiling was a heaven of lapis-lazuli blue. The snow-white Lamb of God rested on a golden sun, surveying us all. The papal throne was also gleaming gold, encrusted with garnets, opals, and topaz. Surrounding the throne were several priests in red and purple vestments. Pope Lucius sat on the throne, dressed all in white. His three-tiered tiara was studded with pearls and diamonds. Gold filigree wove around the gems like a vine. Over his robe was a white chasuble with crosses embroidered in silver and gold. I wished I had worn the damask rose with my fur-lined pelisse. I felt a fool coming into this august company, before the very symbol of Christ on earth, dressed in my third-best gown.

There were several others before us. The pope was

speaking to an Italian noblewoman. Without understanding the Italian words, I heard the pontiff's soft voice offering comfort and guidance. The woman wept and repeated over and over again, "*Grazie, Sua Sanctita.*" The canon translated, "Thank you, Your Holiness."

In that moment I felt filled with peace. This man would hear my plea. I was right to trust him. He would find a way to help me.

At length the Italian noblewoman was dismissed with a benediction. She walked backwards away from the throne. I, too, must remember not to turn my back on the pontiff.

The canon nodded, and Simon let go of my hand. He stepped forward flanked by Brothers Eustace, John, and Aldobert. They each knelt, in turn, and kissed the papal ring. The pope smiled warmly. His kind face was nearly as white as his vestments, and soft looking. It is a face of love and wisdom, I thought.

The canon took a portfolio from Brother Aldobert, opened and presented it to His Holiness. Pope Lucius extracted a sheaf of parchment and held it reverently in his soft white hands. His gentle eyes became bright. We all waited breathlessly for his word.

"*Bello!*" he said at last. "*Bellissimo!*"

"Beautiful, says His Holiness," reported the canon. "He is most pleased."

Even I knew that. How could he not be pleased? Simon was a genius. Still, I was relieved to hear the words of praise. Simon bowed his head. I was so glad for my little brother.

The pope showed Simon's work to the priests who smiled and exclaimed at its beauty. "*Bello!*" I heard again. "*Bellissimo!*"

Now the canon looked at me. It was my turn. Dame Joan, Rhiannon, and I came forward. Simon introduced us to His Holiness, then stepped back. The canon translated.

I bowed low before the pontiff, and kissed his ring. It was very important not to kiss the hand, nor touch His Holiness. I was terrified of stumbling onto the pontiff. Yet the moment passed without incident.

Dame Joan put out her hand for me to steady her. I felt the groan of her knees as she knelt before the pope. Rhiannon dipped so swiftly and gracefully, it hardly seemed she'd made obeisance. We stood back. The pope welcomed us to Rome. Then just as he began to raise his right hand in benediction, I knelt before him in supplication. Dame Joan gasped, and I caught a glimpse of weariness on the pope's face, yet I proceeded.

"Holy Father, I seek your help," I said. "I am pursued by a suitor, but I cannot remarry." It wasn't what I'd meant to say, and I dared not look up as the canon translated.

Without the slightest hesitation, the pope spoke.

"*Povera donna,*" he said in Italian, then continued, much to my surprise in my language. "Poor woman, I hear your unspoken sorrow. You have rightly come to the Mother Church for your protection and salvation."

A flood of grateful tears coursed down my face. Even my inadequate words were heard and understood by His Holiness.

"I shall personally arrange for your admission to the convent of the Good Sisters of St. Cecilia on the morrow. And you may bring your ladies with you."

What! What had he said? My tears ceased, and my heart and head began to pound. I looked up, too shocked for speech. No! I hadn't come to Rome to be immured in a convent. Oh Lord, no!

Rhiannon kicked me, and I found my tongue.

"Your Holiness is most kind," I said. "But I . . . I must fulfill my vow. I must continue my pilgrimage to the Holy Land."

"Ah, yes," said the pontiff. "And when you return to us, St. Cecilia will be ready to receive you."

Pope Lucius blessed us all, and it was time to leave. I rose, benumbed. Rhiannon pulled me backwards out of the hall.

She led me so swiftly out of the palace, we were nearly running. Dame Joan and the brothers lagged far behind us.

Rhiannon dragged me into the shadow of the sun god.

"What *ever* were you thinking?"

"I thought the pope could help me," I said.

"It is you who have helped him."

"What?"

"Pope Lucius wants Simon. Once you are planted in Rome, he may very well get Simon to stay, too."

"Oh."

" 'Oh' isn't enough. And no swoons, nor fevers. You must get us away from here."

"Aye, that I shall do."

XII.
The *Pilgrim's Star*

"You realize that the Good Sisters of St. Cecilia have nothing in common with the Vestal Virgins," said Rhiannon.

"I know that," I said.

"But I've been there," said Rhiannon.

She had the same look of terror that I'd seen when I rescued her from the king's forest.

"You won't go back." I tried to speak firmly, as if filled with conviction. Yet I was just as terrified as Rhiannon, and she knew it.

I had new dreams, more frightening than ever. In them, I ran and ran, but it was never fast enough. I could not escape. I heard the plaintive cry of the kitten, and a kind voice saying: "*Povera donna,* come to me. Be safe with me."

"Where are you?" I called.

"Here I am," said Will Belet at the open gate of a castle.

Before I could get to him, where I knew I'd be safe, a soft white hand reached out of the darkness. I whirled around to find Sir Runcival, and I was trapped.

"Nooooo!" I screamed, and woke.

Rhiannon was at my side, holding me, shushing me. "Don't wake Dame Joan," she whispered in my ear.

I stifled my cries and we rocked each other until sleep came, and I dreamed it all again.

Within the week I arranged to leave Rome. Dame Joan was also glad to depart, though fretful about undertaking the journey ahead of us. She didn't say much to me about our audience with Pope Lucius. Yet I could tell that the pope's plan for us had alarmed her, too.

"I could not live out my days amongst pagans," she said. And I knew she meant the Good Sisters of St. Cecilia.

I wished I could have stayed longer in Rome. I was becoming accustomed to the strangeness of it. I loved the crowded narrow streets that gave way to vast squares, called piazzas. I was especially fond of the giant domed building, the Church of Mary, Mother of all Saints, once called the Pantheon. According to Simon's guidebook, the dome of the Pantheon had been topped with a giant pine cone of solid gold. When the church was consecrated, it was removed, and nothing replaced it. Now there was just a great round hole looking up at the sky. That window to the heavens was what I liked best.

It was cruel to part so soon from Simon. He had to finish his work for Pope Lucius and then return to Godstone. I wondered when I would see my brother again. Did I dare return to England? Would I spend the rest of my days in Jerusalem, or in endless journeying? Oh, peregrine, would you never find a safe roost? Homesickness was catching up with me. When I left England I hadn't thought about returning. Now, I saw that, in order to elude Sir Runcival, I might not be able to go back. I might never see my family, or England, again.

The morning we were to take our leave of Simon and the brothers, they met us at the Lateran gate with five laden mules.

"What is this?" I asked.

"We're going with you!" said Simon.

Even Brother Aldobert was beaming.

"His Most Gracious Holiness has given us permission to accompany you to the Holy Land," said Brother Eustace.

It took Dame Joan a moment to grasp what he'd said. She looked from each to each, uncomprehending.

Simon spoke gently, "It's true. We're all going together."

She threw herself on him.

"Bless you, my little imp, my darling," she cried. "Bless His Holiness for answering my prayers."

Poor Old Wobbly Chins. Why did I ever take her away from England?

Once we were under way, our train headed by Sir Raymond and brought up by the mules, their drivers, and three stout yeomen, I was able to get a private word with Simon.

"How did you manage this?" I asked.

"I simply told His Holiness that you were in need of spiritual guidance, best provided by me and the brothers of Godstone Abbey."

"I see. You are to make sure I return to Rome, to be walled up in St. Cecilia's."

"Yes," he said, grinning. "That is my duty. Unfortunately I shall fail at it miserably."

"You will?"

Simon regarded me with rare seriousness.

"You were not meant for the cloister, Edith," he said. "The Lord has other plans for you."

"I wish you could tell me what those plans might be."

"It will become clear," said Simon. "Keep your heart open to Him, and do not be afraid."

When did my little brother become so sage? Perhaps the cloister had taught him something other than his art. It was something I ought to have learned in Woburn Abbey, but I was too busy vexing the nuns to pay heed to Him.

Simon began to giggle, once more my little brother.

"What?" I asked.

"I also promised His Holiness I'd fill his Psalter with the wonders of Jerusalem."

"So that is the real reason His Holiness let you come."

"It may be the pope's real reason for letting me come," said Simon. "But you are my real reason."

The whole long way over the Apennines and south to the port of Bari, where we'd take passage for the Holy Land, I tried to puzzle out what plan the Lord might have for me. Had my life so far been part of His plan? If that were true, what was the meaning of the death of my little babe? I knew that babies died. Babies, children, mothers, fathers, husbands — all died. Yet, no matter how I pondered it, I could not make sense of it. Perhaps my answer awaited in Jerusalem.

My pilgrimage had begun with the simple need to leave England. I hadn't really cared where I was going as long as it was some place different from where I'd been, and beyond the reach of Sir Runcival of Surrey. I set out for the Holy Land because it was the farthest from England that I could go. I wasn't led by faith. I'd never really listened to anything that the sisters had taught me at Woburn Abbey. Perhaps if I had, I'd not be so despairing now. I had suffered from fevers and chills, but it was the eclipse of my soul that most needed doctoring.

We arrived at Bari, a seaport embedded in cliffs, just in time to board the *Pilgrim's Star* bound for the Outremer. We'd sail from Bari to Joppa, following a circuitous route, picking up and delivering cargo and passengers at many ports. It was a journey of some three weeks. Joppa was only two days' distance from Jerusalem. We'd be in The Holy City by mid August. The object of my travels was very near, especially considering all the weary miles behind us. Yet achieving the Holy City was not a certainty. We'd often been warned that this last sea crossing was the most dangerous of all. We'd heard many stories of tempests and Saracen pirates who preyed on pilgrim ships. Those who were lucky died quickly, those less so were sold into slavery.

We were a crowd of some hundred or more on the *Pilgrim's Star.* All the pilgrims, men and women, were crammed together into the ship's belly with all their possessions and the ship's cargo. The captain was used to dealing with difficult travelers, and remained unmoved by my pleas for a place on deck. Even Sir Raymond was useless against him. Once we'd signed our contract for safe passage, the captain had little patience with our requests. In fair weather we might take the air, only if we didn't interfere with the crew. Men dined at table on deck. Women ate at their berths. Any food other than the bread, mutton, and pudding served were to be provided by the pilgrim. Naturally, bedding and medicines were also our responsibility. The captain had sworn to protect us from the crew, who looked quite capable of violence. Protecting our possessions was up to us.

"And I've heard that to put down one's cup in order to eat one's meat, is to lose the cup," said Dame Joan.

At least the *Pilgrim's Star* was a big, solid-seeming ship. It was kept a sight cleaner than that tub, the *Sea Spray*, that had carried us across the channel.

We arranged our belongings as best we could in the few feet of space that was ours for the voyage. Rhiannon, Dame Joan, and I sat on the traveling chests. The brothers sat on crates filled with our supplies. Our bedding was tied up in bundles and hung just above our heads. Around us the other pilgrims were in small groups, though some traveled in bands of two-score or more. There were so many different types of people: tall, fair, short, dark, thin, fat, old, and young from all over Europe, speaking a multitude of languages. But they all wore the white cross of the pilgrim on their worn and soiled cloaks. Outwardly, I was the same. Did I also share the look of hope I saw in their eyes?

The oarsmen beat the water. Soon the sails caught the wind and we were off.

We were sturdier travelers now. There were no signs of seasickness in any of us. Yet I worried for my old nurse. The traveling grew ever harder for her. The strangeness of the lands we passed through seemed to worry her terribly. Only when she was lost in conversation with Brother Eustace about "home," did Dame Joan seem free from care.

Even though Rhiannon and I tried to hide my night

demons from her, Dame Joan woke often enough to know that I was still troubled. I know she worried for my sake. But during the day, we didn't speak about the terrors of the nights. None of us spoke of Sir Runcival, nor Pope Lucius. I hadn't the nerve to ask Simon more about Will. And neither Simon nor Rhiannon spoke of him. But often I thought of Will. I wondered where he was. Had he left yet for England? If ever he was near Wallingford, he'd call upon my family. Father would surely speak of my pilgrimage. Then Will might think of me. Perhaps he was thinking of me now.

A woman commenced to wail from the far corner of the hold.

"Merciful Lord!" she cried. "Show these sinners the error of their ways."

I recognized that voice; so did Dame Joan. She looked at me, eyes wide.

"It could not be," she said.

"Praise the Lord!" shrieked the woman, and began sobbing loudly.

"Lord help us," I said.

"What is it?" asked Simon.

"*It* is a most tiresome, noisy woman, Dame Margery Kempe, who is full sure of her own holiness," said Dame Joan in disgust.

"A holy woman in our midst," said Brother John, brightly. "Is it not a good omen?"

"*No!*" Dame Joan and I said it in unison. Simon and

the brothers looked at us, confused. But Rhiannon clapped her hands, and laughed.

"Do not worry," she told Dame Joan. "I will protect you from the holy woman."

If only she could have. As the days aboard ship passed, Dame Margery proved to be a greater nuisance than the flies. At least I could swat at flies.

"What have I not suffered on this Holy Pilgrimage?" wailed Dame Margery at the midday meal. "But the Lord knows, I shall find my reward in heaven."

"Would that you find your reward soon," muttered Dame Joan.

One of the pilgrim women came forward and silently implored Rhiannon to do something. Rhiannon was the only one aboard ship able to silence Dame Margery. She walked resolutely to Dame Margery's corner, and spoke quietly in her ear. Dame Margery blanched, and closed her mouth.

"What did you tell her?" I asked.

"Nothing," she said, smiling smugly. But somehow she frightened "Saint" Margery into a half-hour of blessed silence.

Dame Margery seemed especially attracted to Dame Joan and me. Whenever Rhiannon was up on deck with Simon, she made straight for us.

"I see the mark of the Lord upon you," she said, pointing her freckled finger at me. "He is testing you, Lady Edith. Will you be worthy?"

No. I was not worthy. But why should He test me?

"Pray over someone else," said Dame Joan. "Leave my lady in peace."

"Only in the Lord is there peace," said Dame Margery. "Only in the Lord!"

I wanted to ignore her. Wasn't she just an overbearing fool? And yet, she seemed so very certain, knowing without doubts, the Lord's plan for her.

We had brief respite from Dame Margery, the fleas, the stifling heat, and the putrid smells of rotting food, sweat, and urine when the ship docked at the various ports along our way. We paid a fortune to be rowed ashore. Only the poorest pilgrims remained aboard the ship.

I loved the new seas and the new lands. Each place seemed more extraordinary than the last, but the captain was always in such a rush to reach the next port of call, we had time for little more than the most fleeting impressions. Simon worked frantically to sketch what he saw. I tried to capture one clear picture of each place to store away in my mind. Back aboard the stinking ship I'd borrow a leaf of parchment from Simon and try to put my pictures into words. There was the stark Greek island of white rock sheering up out of the blue-as-cornflower sea, the Dalmatian church, from the outside as dwarfed and stunted as a cave, holding within mosaics more dazzling than a king's crown. I thought of the Tibors and wrestled with my words to make them match the images in my head.

Constantinople was more exquisite than anything we'd seen before. We were there for only one short afternoon, and raced across the city to see the Basilica of St. Sophia. It was a wonder. Hundreds of marble columns supported the great dome. And nearly every inch of wall and ceiling was covered with frescoes and mosaics of such intense colors, I was nearly blinded by them. We had to drag Simon out of the church, and he was in tears as the oarsmen pulled us away from the city.

"You'll go back," I said. "The pope will need a complete record of Byzantium."

He brightened a little.

As much as by the new places, I was fascinated by the people: tawny, and ebon-colored skin, women wrapped in layers of veils so that only their shining black eyes were visible, and beggars with nothing more than a rag over their groins. Yet as different as these people were from those of England, I kept seeing amongst them faces that might have belonged to the villeins of Cheswick or Wallingford. How could that be?

Dame Joan found it very difficult. She left the ship only to get away from its miseries. Once on land the foreign smells and voices, the oddly shaped houses, the weight of the sun — all threw her off-balance. She actually stumbled, and would fall if Brother Eustace wasn't there to uphold her.

Rhiannon seemed to be living a dream. She walked about, her eyes deep wells seeing everything. She never spoke on land. She'd not waste herself in words. Only on shipboard did she speak. Then she astonished me with torrents, recalling every step she'd taken, every sight she'd seen. I showed Rhiannon my word pictures.

"Lady Edith," she said. "You didn't tell me that the *trobairitz* had taught you their art."

"Well," I said.

"Do not blush and dissemble," said Rhiannon. "You are as skilled with words as your brother is with his paints and brushes. You must write more about your travels, and all that you've seen."

The Tibors had given me a gift. I would cherish it; I would use it.

Rhiannon smiled.

"Yes," I said. "Yes, I will write."

Eventually we came to the coast of Palestine. We gathered on the deck and sang the Lord's praise at our first sight of the Holy Land. The massive stone fortress of Acre was blazing white against the startling blue sky. There were no soft colors here, no blurred edges. Everything was stark, stripped to its essence: bleached stones, burnt earth, blue sky. Must I also be so exposed?

"Be joyful," said Rhiannon. "Having come this far is enough for now."

Dame Margery disembarked at Acre. With luck, we might never see her again. An ancient Norseman, named Saewulf, took her place. His much-patched cape was covered with the badges of earlier pilgrimages. There were scallop shells from St. James of Compostela in Spain, palms from Jerusalem, and badges I didn't recognize from many other shrines. His skin was burnished and pleated, and his hair stood out from his head, a wild crown of hoarfrost. He sat on his pilgrim's gear, glaring at all around him. At length he began to speak. The pilgrims gathered to hear him tell the tale of his first voyage to Jerusalem, some forty years before. I held back with Dame Joan, wary of his gaze.

"I was in my full strength then," said Saewulf. "And I needed every ounce of it to survive."

He paused to blow his nose on his sleeve.

"A storm, such as only the Mediterranean can brew, burst upon us. The pilgrim ship was lifted out of the water by the wicked winds and wrecked upon the shore near Joppa. Only I and some two score other souls survived."

His bleached eyes challenged us from the shadow of his brow, as if any amongst us would dare contradict him.

"Barely our clothes were dry, we began the trek across the thirsty hills from Joppa to Jerusalem.

"Bands of Saracens hid in those hills, in every rocky

hollow and cave. Woe to a pilgrim band not able to protect itself. Any straggler was doomed. The heathens swarmed out of their lairs, slaughtering the weak. They stripped away anything of value and left their naked victims for the scavenging beasts. Oh, the number of human bones these eyes have seen, along the road to Jerusalem."

In Saewulf's wild eyes I saw a vision of our own poor selves as savaged carrion. When I left England I had no use for life. Now I couldn't stand the thought of dying before I'd reached my goal. Something awaited me in Jerusalem, some reckoning, and I didn't want to miss it.

The ship groaned and creaked. Up on deck were the shouts of the sailors and the stamp of their heavy boots. Below no one spoke, nor stirred. Next to me Dame Joan was shivering. I wrapped her in my cloak and tried to rub comfort into her old bones.

Rhiannon, of all people, broke the spell.

"That is an old tale," she said. "'Tis good for frightening babes at night. The Knights Templar and the Hospitallers have made the ways to Jerusalem safer than the King's Road from London to Kent."

"Aye," said Saewulf. "They did, but new trouble's afoot."

Rhiannon stared the old man down. "There is always new trouble," she said. "It won't matter in the least to these pilgrims."

Was she trying to comfort Dame Joan, or me? It was still rare for her to speak in private. I'd never before heard Rhiannon volunteer anything in public. We were all changing in unaccountable ways. I didn't like it. The ground was shifting too much under my feet.

"Such a slip of a girl," said a fat friar. "Yet such a prodigious mouth."

Some laughed.

"She's got more sense than many of us," said Simon. "We do not go to Jerusalem in fear, but in joy."

I wished I could have felt that way. I was one of the ones without sense.

Dame Joan tugged on my sleeve and looked at me with round fearful eyes. "We'll die, won't we?" she said. "The Saracens will murder us."

I petted her, and kissed her worried brow. "Don't worry," I said. "Sir Raymond will be always at our side."

She nodded, but I could see that compared to Saewulf's tale, my comfort was a paltry thing. I wished I could allay her fears; I wished I could allay my own.

XIII.
Judah ben Avram

As we approached the port of Joppa the sea was more aquamarine than any place else I'd been. The water eased up to gently caress white sand beaches. The old Norseman's tale of murderous tempests seemed absurd. This docile sea wasn't capable of an ugly wave.

When the port officials were through with us, we were finally released from the stagnant belly of the *Pilgrim's Star.* Straight away, Rhiannon leapt onto her mare and raced into the sea. Horse and maid swam together while we watched from the shore.

"It's scandalous," Brother Eustace said. Brothers John and Aldobert condemned her silently. Rhiannon emerged from the water, dripping and beatific, and I couldn't be angry with her. Dame Joan said nothing, which gave me more to wonder about than Rhiannon's rashness.

We had two days of travel ahead of us before reaching Jerusalem. We were so close, I wanted to fly as fast as I might to the Holy City and to whatever awaited me there. At the same time, I wanted to hold back. Once my journey was over I'd have to decide what my life was to be. Dared I return to England, and risk being in thrall to Sir Runcival? Would I have to remain on foreign shores? And if so, where? Oh, peregrine!

"This is only your first morning in the Holy Land," said Rhiannon. "You haven't allowed anything to happen, yet."

Her hair was blowing loose and her face was an open flower.

"You are a pretty sea sprite," I said.

"Now look who has become the evasive one," she said, and kissed me.

We'd landed at dawn, when it was relatively cool. But the heat built through the day and began to weigh on us as heavy as iron. On the Via Maris, the sea road, Mediterranean breezes brought some relief from the burning sun. Palms were planted along the way and their shade was a blessing. All of us, except Sir Raymond, wore large white platters on our heads, hats we'd acquired at the Joppa quay. They looked ridiculous, especially on the brothers, but any protection from the sun was welcome.

That night we camped on the shore. Rhiannon and I waded into the moonlit water in our shifts. After much coaxing, I lured Dame Joan into the warm sea.

" 'Tis only to wash away the filth of the ship," she said. "I won't enjoy it at all."

Soon she was floating in the sea and smiling serenely.

I heard splashing and hoots of laughter from where Simon was bathing with Peter and the brothers. I didn't imagine Brother Aldobert or Brother John would allow themselves such merriment. Perhaps Brother Eustace had indulged in a moment of fun. Sir Raymond stood guard. For once I felt safe and at peace. I floated in the water and recited the names of all the places we'd been to.

"Godstone, Dover, Boulogne, St. Denis, Paris, Vezelay . . ."

Rhiannon joined in and our list of travels became a song. *"Lyons, Sarenom, Marseilles, Rome, Bari, Dalmatia, Greece, Constantinople . . ."* What a long way I'd come to bathe contentedly.

It didn't last. When the sun came up and we headed away from the beautiful sea into the scorched hills I recalled every terrifying word of Saewulf's tale. I saw the brown hills pockmarked with caves, sheltering hundreds of murderers. A skulking fox, and the piebald crows keening above, were just waiting for the chance to pick clean our bones. Bedouin shepherds, leading their bedraggled flocks in search of the rare bit of grass, became deadly stalkers. Not even the presence of Hospitaller knights patrolling the roads calmed my fears.

Rhiannon eased her mare next to mine on the narrow path.

"Stop it!" she said in a harsh whisper. "Every time you startle at nothing, you unnerve Dame Joan."

I glanced over my shoulder. Dame Joan was ghostly white and trembling. Rhiannon was right. I had to control myself and help Dame Joan. I let Rhiannon go ahead of me and fell back beside my old nurse.

"The sun is strong," I ventured. "Does it trouble you?"

"Nay," said Dame Joan. " 'Tis not the sun."

I knew that, but I was trying to get us away from dark, shadowy things.

"These hats are quite helpful," I said.

"Aye," she said.

"Though I'll be glad of fresh water when we get to Jerusalem, won't you?"

"Hmm!"

She was becoming as close-mouthed as Rhiannon. "I hear the water is sweet in the Holy City."

Dame Joan sat straighter in her saddle and glared at me. "If you want water now, fetch it yourself. Or go and nag Peter. I have other concerns."

"I'm sorry . . ."

"Hmph!" She spurred her horse, and drew ahead of me.

I wondered why she was so angry with me. Whatever it was, at least for the moment, she seemed to have stopped worrying about Saracen marauders. I dropped back to Simon, who was enduring a sermon from Brother Eustace.

"In this way we can know Christ's presence . . ."

"I beg your pardon, Brother Eustace," I said. "Be so

good as to accompany Dame Joan. I believe she needs your assistance."

"If you think I can be of service?"

"You alone," I said.

He hastened to catch up with her, which wasn't easy in the heat and over the rocky ground.

"Thank heaven for sweet deliverance," said Simon.

"You're welcome," I said. "Now help me."

"Anything, Lady Edith."

"I *am* worried about Dame Joan. Have you noted how differently she's been acting of late?"

Simon looked uncomfortable. After a moment he said, "I don't really know her as well as you."

"Simon, for shame! Not know the woman who bullied, scrubbed, and coddled you from birth?"

He sighed. "You're right. She has changed. And I don't like it."

"What's to be done?"

"What can be done? She is old and tired, and . . ." he trailed off.

"And I've given her a good deal to worry about."

"Yes."

He was right. It was largely my doing. Now I couldn't meet Simon's eye, and studied the haze of sea on the road behind us. If I'd brought about this change in Dame Joan with my own troubles, then I'd have to set things right. I'd start by convincing her that I was well and happy. Whether or not it was true made little difference. Perhaps in Jerusalem I would also find an answer to this problem. If only I could approach the Lord with an untroubled heart.

I looked back toward Simon in time to see a shadow separate itself from the larger shadow of a rock outcropping, and slide onto the path before me. My horse shied. Simon shouted to Sir Raymond. I heard Dame Joan shriek. The shadow sank to the ground, a substantial pile of rags and dust.

I got control of my mare, and tried to command my pounding heart. Sir Raymond halted our train, and came thundering back to me.

"Honored Lady, I mean no harm," said the cowering form. "I am Judah ben Avram. I am a good guide. I can show you everything in the holy city. I know everyone. I can get you the best prices."

I was too unnerved by his sudden appearance to risk speech.

Sir Raymond was at my side. "What's this?" he said.

"A guide," said Simon.

"A Saracen assassin!" said Dame Joan, drawing close behind me.

"No, Esteemed Mistress, I am a Jew."

In all the long way from England to here, this was the first Jew I'd ever been this close to. Yet he seemed not much different than other men. He was heavily bearded, and of great girth. Beneath the dust his robes were of fine colored silk.

Rhiannon came up beside me. Her eyes twinkled with mirth. "Doesn't this remind you of another supplicant?" She spoke softly for me alone to hear.

Yes, it was uncomfortably familiar — too much like her own first appearance in my life. I only hoped Judah ben Avram wouldn't be as perplexing as Rhiannon.

"Is he armed?" asked Dame Joan. "Is he alone?"

"Honored Lady," said Judah ben Avram, speaking to me, "I am only one."

"Others might be hiding," Dame Joan persisted.

"He is just one old man," said Simon.

"How can you be so sure?" asked Dame Joan. "You can't believe an infidel, a killer of Christ."

Sir Raymond cleared his throat and spoke. "The Hospitallers told me that a guide can be quite useful. They barter with the natives, get the best prices for food and lodging. We'd need to hire one once we reached Jerusalem."

"Yes, yes, wise Sir Knight. A guide is good, and I am the best guide."

"Do you think this one will do?" I asked.

Sir Raymond shrugged his massive shoulders. I looked to Simon.

"Ask how much he charges," he said.

"Just four small silver coins each new moon," said Judah ben Avram.

"A silver penny a week, that's too much!" said Dame

Joan, sounding like her old self for the first time in weeks.

"What do you think he should get?" I asked her.

"The heathen will make a profit on every transaction he arranges for us. I don't think we should pay him anything."

Judah ben Avram's ample face broke into a wide grin.

"Esteemed Mistress is very clever," he said. "It will be a great pleasure to serve her."

"You see," said Dame Joan. "That's the way to treat them!"

"Ah, but Esteemed Mistress will not let a poor old man starve." Judah ben Avram hadn't finished with his bartering. "Two small pieces of silver at the new moon."

"One silver penny," said Dame Joan. "Take it or leave it!"

"I will remain a poor man," said Judah ben Avram. "But I cannot refuse." He clasped his hands as in prayer, and bowed three times.

"That was artful," said Rhiannon in my ear.

He had gotten us to take him on. In the process Dame Joan had recovered her wits, and her humor. Perhaps Judah ben Avram had been sent especially to spar with her, to help Dame Joan keep her balance in this strange land.

Rhiannon was grinning at me.

"What?" I asked.

"Judah ben Avram will be Dame Joan's nettle, as I am yours," she whispered.

I stopped and stared at her. Was that it? Was Rhiannon my nettle? To what purpose? To goad me into what action?

Rhiannon smiled at me, as ever reading the words inside my head. Had God sent her to me? Was He indeed sending Judah ben Avram to Dame Joan? If only I could believe that it all had some meaning. I felt the weary weight of this day and all the others going all the way back to the day of my betrothal. Dame Joan, Sir Raymond, and Simon were looking to me. They seemed to be waiting for me to say something. Oh yes. It was for me to confirm what had already been decided.

"It is settled," I said. "Judah ben Avram will be our guide."

"A thousand blessings on your house," he said, and rose from the ground with surprising agility. He straightened his robes, shaking out more dust. "Now I will take you to a *wadi* where you will sleep well this night."

The sun was showing faint signs of relenting. Soon we would have to consider finding a place to water the horses, and shelter for the night. If Judah ben Avram was indeed our guide, this would be a good test of his resourcefulness. Yet I felt wary of following this stranger, this Jew, away from the road into God-knew-what circumstances. Would he lead us to a well, or to slaughter?

Rhiannon was glaring at me. Why? Because I did not fully trust this Jew?

"Yes," she said. "Mean-spiritedness and distrust ill become you."

I tried to create a blank wall in my mind that Rhiannon could not penetrate. And she laughed out loud.

"Don't try any tricks," said Dame Joan to Judah ben Avram. "I'll be watching you every minute, and Sir Raymond will run you through at the first sign of trouble."

"Not to worry, Esteemed Mistress," he replied. "We are all in God's hands."

"Are we?" I hadn't meant to say that, certainly not to this complete stranger.

Judah ben Avram looked at me kindly, seeming undaunted by my irreverence. "Most assuredly, Honored Lady," he said. "You are in God's safekeeping."

If only I could believe that.

XIV.
The Bedouin Camp

We continued along the road for a short while before Judah ben Avram led us down a shepherd's track into a fold of the hills. There soon appeared a trickling stream, and a small grove of palms and acacias. After our day in the brown hills, the sound of water and the sight of green was glorious. My mare perked up as she smelled the water. Beside the stream was a shepherd's camp.

"We can't stay here," said Dame Joan. "These are Arabs; they'll murder us in our sleep."

"No, Esteemed Mistress," soothed Judah ben Avram. "This is the camp of a Bedouin chief. He will receive you most graciously."

"Receive us!" said Dame Joan. "I'm not going into that filthy tent."

The large, sprawling, mud-brown tent set amidst the sheep and donkeys did seem about as appealing as a sheep byre.

"Esteemed Mistress must not be deceived by outward appearances."

We were now too far advanced to retreat. The horses needed to rest. We all did, Dame Joan more than any of us. It was up to me to be decisive, and firm.

"We must trust our guide," I said, and looked to Rhiannon.

"Yes," she said.

"Sir Raymond will see to our safety," I added, and urged my mare forward. Judah ben Avram hurried along beside me.

"Honored Lady . . ." he began.

"You may call me Lady Edith. My companions are Dame Joan and Mistress Rhiannon. Brother Simon will introduce you to the other holy brothers traveling with us."

"Honored Lady Edith is kind and wise," he said.

"Do not lead us astray," I said.

I rode up to the tent. Judah ben Avram helped me dismount, and steadied me until my legs could function properly. All my life I'd been taught that Jews, the killers of Christ, were horned demons. I'd never thought about it until now. I'd never known a Jew. Judah ben Avram didn't look much like an Englishman, yet he wasn't all that different from dark-eyed Brother Aldobert. He might have been Provençal or Italian. His touch reminded me of my father's, solid and comforting.

Soon everyone else caught up with us.

Our arrival caused a flurry of activity in the Bedouin camp. Almond-eyed children ran around us, giggling and tugging at our robes. Their mothers peeked out from their veils, hanging back in the shadow of the tent. The men seemed guarded.

"Please come with me," said Judah ben Avram, and he strode into the tent.

I made sure Sir Raymond was behind me, then followed him in.

I stopped in my tracks, astonished; inside, the tent was beautiful and elegant. Silk and wool carpets in brilliant reds and blues covered every inch of ground and hung all along the sides. A soft golden light shone from dozens of hanging brass lamps. The Bedouin chief, dressed in snowy linen, reclined on a mound of silk and damask cushions. All was immaculate, smelling sweetly of spice and incense. An image of Oxford Castle came suddenly to mind. There the rushes were often rank with dog droppings and rotting food. Knights and squires came in from the hunt, mud-splattered and pungent. How different it was in this "sheep byre."

The others came in behind me, and I heard someone gasp. I turned to see Dame Joan with eyes as round as saucers.

"You see," said Rhiannon.

Simon looked delighted. Peter and the holy brothers seemed stunned. It shamed me to be so surprised at finding this civilized haven. And it shamed me again that we were the uncouth invaders, coming in dust-covered and travel-worn.

"*Salaam alekum,*" said Judah ben Avram.

The Bedouin chief murmured his reply.

Judah ben Avram continued speaking unhurriedly in the strange tongue. I heard him say my name, and I bowed to the white-robed chief. He regarded me with heavily lidded eyes and nodded.

At length he spoke, slowly, deeply, his arms drawing expansive arcs in the air. Clearly he was offering his hospitality. I bowed again, and he smiled.

"The most worthy Abdullah ibn Battuta welcomes you to his humble abode," Judah ben Avram translated. "He begs you to accept food, drink, and a soft bed. His servants are your servants. His home is yours."

"Thank the most worthy Abdullah ibn Battuta," I said, trying to emulate the style of Judah ben Avram, and feeling truly grateful.

"It would be most proper if Honored Lady Edith had a gift for our worthy host," said Judah ben Avram.

I could see that a gift would be helpful, but what? Simon came to my side.

"We can give him one of my scrolls," he said.

"Truly, Simon?"

He nodded.

"Peter!"

"Yes, milady."

"Fetch my saddlebag."

Peter raced off and soon returned.

"Please accept this gift." I held out one of the beautiful scrolls Simon had painted of the psalms while he was in Rome. "This is the work of my brother, Illuminator to His Holiness, Pope Lucius."

Simon choked, but recovered himself enough to bow deeply.

Judah ben Avram translated. "This is a painting from the great and holy city of the Latin fathers."

Judah ben Avram presented the scroll. As Abdullah ibn Battuta opened it his eyes grew wide with delight. He laughed aloud and called for others to come and see.

Judah ben Avram beamed at us like a proud parent. "An excellent gift, Honored Lady Edith and Holy Brother Simon. An excellent gift!"

In our honor a sheep was slaughtered and roasted. Dame Joan, Rhiannon, and I were taken behind a curtained wall. Several Bedouin women brought basins of scented water for us to wash away the dust of the road. The women seemed fascinated with our dress, as I was with theirs. They watched intently as Dame Joan and I put on fresh wimples. Rhiannon allowed one of the women to comb out her tangled hair, and plait it.

There seemed to be a discussion about Rhiannon's midnight hair and clear blue eyes. At least there was a lot of pointing and smiling. Once we had changed into less worn, and less dirty robes, we began to look worthy of the Bedouin chief's hospitality.

We returned to the presence of Abdullah ibn Battuta, and sat upon silken cushions. I was pleased to see that Simon, Sir Raymond, and the brothers had taken some pains to tidy themselves. While the meal was being prepared, we were served a hot drink of aromatic herbs and mint. Abdullah ibn Battuta presented Dame Joan, Rhiannon, and me with round silver bracelets set with gemstones.

"How lovely!" said Dame Joan, her eyes shining. "Are they really for us to keep?"

"Certainly to keep," said Judah ben Avram.

"Fancy!" she said and bowed to our host.

The women brought in platters of food, set them on a low table in front of us, then disappeared behind a curtained wall. Children darted in and out, begging for scraps. The men fed them morsels of mutton, pieces of soft flat bread dipped in pungent sauces, olives, nuts, bits of the hard sheep's cheese, dates, and sweet confections of honey, nuts, and spice. Though the children came to be fed, they stayed to satisfy their curiosity.

Once they understood that Simon had painted the beautiful scroll, they swarmed over him, teasing him to produce more such magic. Peter fetched a leaf of parchment, inks, pens, and brushes. Simon was about to sketch one of the children, but Judah ben Avram quickly intervened.

"Revered Holy Brother, it is against the teachings of Muhammed to portray people or animals. Please draw some pretty flowers for the children and show them how you write in your language."

Simon set to work. Soon the parchment was covered with flowers of England. He drew lilies, hyacinths, and roses, and wrote their names in Latin and flowing English. Then he drew the humble flowers of field and forest: daisies, violets, bleeding hearts, foxgloves, feverfew, and camomile. The children crowded around him, shrieking excitedly as each new blossom took shape. Even some of the women became bold enough to linger.

He drew all the sweet familiar flowers of home. I'd never given them much thought before. But now I remembered the flowers, the trees, the green fields of my home. It was so different from this parched, brown land. Would I ever see my home again? Unbidden tears filled my eyes and began to course down my cheeks. I quickly wiped them away and hoped that everyone was too caught up with Simon's drawing to have noticed. I couldn't go back to England. I didn't have to reach Jersualem to know what I'd been knowing all along. As long as Sir Runcival existed, I couldn't go home. Neither could I return to Rome unless I found some way to avoid the pope's designs. There was no sense longing for what I'd lost, for what I couldn't have. Besides, I'd put so much energy into *leaving* England. I didn't want to live beside the graves of my husband and child. I'd come looking for an answer, and had not yet begun to find it. Surely I could be patient, at least until I got to the Holy City.

"Will Belet is in England," Rhiannon's voice whispered in my ear.

I whirled around to face her, and found instead Judah ben Avram. Rhiannon was between Simon and Dame Joan; she wasn't even looking at me.

Judah ben Avram spoke softly to me. "Are you tired?" he asked. "Would you like to go to the women? They will see you to your comfort."

I wanted desperately to go off by myself.

"Yes," I said. "If it won't offend our host, I'd like very much to retire."

"It will not offend." He spoke a few words to Abdullah ibn Battuta. The Bedouin bowed to me, and I to him. A veiled woman appeared instantly, and led me to the curtained wall. Everyone else was still distracted by Simon; not even Dame Joan noticed my departure.

I was taken back beyond the chamber we'd already seen, through a series of small curtained enclosures to one made up with three pallets, and my traveling chest. The woman showed me a pitcher of water and a basin. She pointed out the soft cushions on the pallets and pantomimed sleep. I nodded. She murmured what I took to be a soft benediction. I bowed, and she left me.

I dropped to the nearest pallet, and hid my face in the cool cushion. Was I now hearing Rhiannon's thoughts as clearly as she heard mine? Why was she telling me that Will Belet was in England, when I couldn't go back there? I might remember Will, as I remembered the days of my girlhood. My girlhood and those days were gone. They were only memories. Will's life had gone on without me, as mine had gone on without him. Will Belet was more than a memory. Especially of late, he'd become a living presence. But that didn't mean that he belonged in any way to me. I could not put him into my future. It would probably be best to put him out of my mind.

I spoke the names of my travels to ease me into sleep. "*Godstone, Dover, Boulogne, St. Denis, Paris, Vezelay . . .*" I soon fell into troubled dreams of flowering green hills and the face of Will Belet.

XV.
Montjoye

I woke in the dark, my cheeks wet with tears. My dreams had veered into a land of such sorrow that my tears continued though I hardly remembered what it was I'd dreamed.

Where was I? I'd woken in many strange places, yet this felt the strangest of all. There was not the faintest hint of light, nor breath of air. Was I already in the tomb, having forgotten my own death?

Rhiannon sighed in her sleep, and I remembered. We were in one of the carpeted bowers of the Bedouin's tent. And I'd had a dream of all that I'd lost. I wouldn't sleep again, no matter how far off the morning; I couldn't bear to dream any more.

By today's end we'd be in Jerusalem, the goal of these many weeks of travel. I should have felt relief, or joy, or something other than this cloud of despair. Jerusalem was my final destination, and my last hope. What if it was the end of hope? What if I'd come this far to find nothing?

Rhiannon stirred and I feigned sleep.

"Have you no faith at all?" she asked.

How could she wake from sleep and know the very thing that troubled me?

"Not much," I answered.

"Oughtn't you to trust in the Lord?"

There was something in her voice. She was both teasing and serious.

"Yes, I ought." I could feel her amusement.

"Is it time to get up?" asked Dame Joan, groggily.

Before I could answer, the curtain parted and one of the Bedouin women came in with a flickering candle and a steaming jug.

"*Salaam alekum,*" she said.

"*Salaam alekum,*" I echoed.

The rest of the conversation we managed with pointing and hand signs. It was time to leave. The men were awake and readying the horses.

"Thank you," I said with my hands clasped prayerfully. She smiled, bowed, and left.

We took our leave of Abdullah ibn Battuta with long florid speeches which I couldn't understand, and much bowing. It was still dark, and cool breezes followed us into the morning's light. By midmorning we'd reached the crest of Montjoye and our first sight of Jerusalem.

There it was, atop one of the brown Judean hills. It might have been any bleached white city of the Outremer. There was no golden light emanating from it, nor leading us to it.

"I suppose you expected a halo," said Rhiannon.

"Something," I said. I did expect some sort of sign, at least, some feeling of joy in my own heart.

Sir Raymond approached me.

"Nearly there, milady."

"Indeed, Sir Raymond." It was so unlike him to talk to me. I wondered what this was about.

"Never thought I'd live to see it."

"You didn't?"

"Getting on in years," he said. "Well . . ."

"Yes, Sir Raymond?"

"Crusader kings built it up, fine city," he said. "But . . ."

"But, what?"

"King Baldwin's daughter, Queen Melisende, isn't the man her father was."

I hoped not.

"Have a care, milady," he said, bowed and left my side.

"What was that?" I asked Rhiannon.

"A sign?" she said, teasing me.

We dismounted. Dame Joan, Simon, the holy brothers, Sir Raymond, Peter, and all the men knelt together on the dry brown hill and sang His praises. It was a time to rejoice and give thanks.

"Almighty God, Father of all mercies, we thine unworthy servants do give thee most humble and hearty thanks," intoned Brother John.

"We bless thee for bringing us safely through sickness and danger . . ." Brother Aldobert continued.

Dame Joan had tears streaming down her cheeks. Peter did, too. Even Rhiannon knelt of her own accord. I sank to my knees beside her. Judah ben Avram was lost in prayer. It took me a moment to remember that Jerusalem was a holy city for him, as well. All in our company seemed to feel the grace of His holy presence except me. I felt nothing but the worry and suffocating heaviness I'd carried all the way from England.

Seeing the end of my journey brought me no relief. I'd risked so much for myself, Dame Joan, and the others to come to Jerusalem. Perhaps I'd escaped Sir Runcival. Perhaps I could evade the pope's plan for me. I'd have to wait and see. Soon, soon I'd be in the Heavenly City. It was said that to walk where Jesus Christ had walked and to pray where He had died and arisen would bring the peace that I longed for, but I wasn't hopeful. My worries about Sir Runcival were only a portion of my heart's heaviness. All the sorrow I'd thought well buried and left behind in England had come back sharp and painfully clear in last night's dreams.

All night long I'd had visions of those dear to me, each one bidding me a sad farewell. I'd felt the warmth of Will's hand in mine; then he was gone to the dangers of battle. My husband set out on a long journey. He kissed my cheek with lips already cold. My tiny little daughter, too young to speak, sighed in my arms and began to fade. Within seconds she'd become a gossamer apparition. And then she was gone. Vanished. I called to Dame Joan to come and help me find my child. I called and called, but she never came. No one came.

Since waking I'd just barely managed to keep back my tears. Rhiannon knew to let me be. Somehow she managed to distract Dame Joan. It was easy to avoid Simon, who was suffering more sermons from Brother Eustace as we continued on to Jerusalem. Left alone I might have been able to gain some composure, but Judah ben Avram was ever at my side. Why wasn't he with Dame Joan? Wasn't he meant to be her goad? I already had Rhiannon, Simon, and my own relentless conscience. Yet I couldn't get away from him; the track was too treacherous to spur on my mare. Often I had to dismount and walk as we negotiated a sharp descent or climb. Then I was truly at his mercy.

"Honored Lady Edith, you are troubled this day?"

I shook my head.

"I see it in your eyes. What great sorrow could afflict one so young?"

"Nothing," I said. "I am merely travel weary."

"Travel makes one tired, not sad," he said.

I tried to distract myself, to remain dry-eyed. I studied the ribbons of cypress trees clinging to the brown slopes. Could this parched land really be what the ancients called "The Land of Milk and Honey"? The land of milk and honey become desert. That was my story. The dream of my daughter came back to me. I felt again the joy of holding her, followed by the terrible emptiness of holding nothing. It was as clear and horrible as when it actually happened so many months ago. A sob escaped me.

"What is it?" Judah ben Avram would not let me be.

"I've been troubled by dreams," I said. "That is all."

"Dream are messages the All-Knowing God sends to us. If we pay close heed, our dreams will reveal His plan."

I wanted to believe him. Even if I did, what sense was there in last night's dreams?

"I see you don't believe me," he said.

Another mind reader! Wasn't it bad enough to have Rhiannon always poking around inside my head? Now there'd be this infidel, as well.

Judah ben Avram bowed low. "Honored Lady Edith, I mean no harm. We both believe in the One God, yes?"

I nodded.

"Do we agree that the One God created the world and everything in it?"

"Yes."

"And He has given it all to mankind?"

I thought back to the dimly remembered lessons of the nuns at Woburn Abbey about the creation of the world. Were these the same stories Judah ben Avram knew?

"The Almighty God has given us the sun, the moon, the earth bearing fresh fruits, creatures of the land and air, and seas teeming with fish. The air we breathe, the water that quenches thirst, all that will sustain and delight us, He has given."

How could one so seemingly different from Brother Eustace sound so much like him? I did not want to pursue this discussion any further, but there was no way to escape Judah ben Avram.

We were nearing the city walls, and were no longer a small company on a lonely road. We'd become part of a great stream of animals and people snaking up the steep road to the walled city. The great stone portal to Jerusalem was only a short distance ahead.

"The God of Abraham, Isaac, and Jacob did not create the earth and all its bounty that Honored Lady Edith should walk in sorrow."

"Neither did He create the world that *I* might be happy."

"Honored Lady Edith, being happy is part of God's plan. He gave us so much, why shouldn't we be happy?"

God's plan. Did God's plan really include my happiness?

"Honored Lady Edith," Judah ben Avram began.

"What now?" I snapped.

"Look, we are approaching the Damascus Gate."

I sat up higher on my horse and looked over the throng in front of us. Yes. There it was, so very close. The portal to the earthly Jerusalem, the entry to the celestial city. My heart seemed to start beating. I felt that I was at once leaving myself and returning to life. I drew a deep breath of the scorching air.

Judah ben Avram smiled up at me. "That is better, Honored Lady Edith. The Almighty God now sees your happiness and smiles with you."

That was quite a thought, the Almighty God smiling with Lady Edith of Cheswick! I nearly laughed out loud.

A caravan of camels and stocky little donkeys was a few yards ahead of us. I'd seen a number of camels since we'd landed in Joppa, but not yet been so close to them. They were wonderfully strange and ugly. Brightly patterned blankets covered their humps. Knotted fringe, tassels, and bells hung from silver pommels on the saddles and from the reins. The best dressed beasts carried men swathed in equally gorgeous silks and brocades, their heads wrapped in elaborate turbans. They perched on the high saddles, lurching from side to side with the camels' odd loping gait. I was glad, as ever, to be on my dainty mare, yet shamed by my drab and dusty pilgrim's garb. How much better it would have been to enter Jerusalem as resplendent as a rainbow.

Although I was somberly dressed, I felt a spark of color growing inside me. I had the sensation that something awaited me in Jerusalem besides my own gloominess.

"Lady Edith!" called Dame Joan.

I reined in my mare and waited for her to catch up with me.

"Why ever are you grinning like an ape? We are about to enter the Holy City. It is not seemly to be mirthful."

I nodded, and tried to put on a more sober face.

"Brother Eustace says that we should dismount and walk humbly through the gate."

"All right," I said.

Rhiannon wouldn't like it. I don't think she minded walking so much as being parted from her horse. She might have been one of those pagan centaurs we'd seen in the ancient mosaics of Rome. She rode up to us and leapt lightly from her saddle without even a grimace of protest. Rhiannon had become strangely compliant of late, especially toward Dame Joan. I should have been pleased, but it seemed that her deference to Dame Joan marked some further decline in my old nurse, and it worried me.

Soon the holy brothers were walking with us up the final slope to the Damascus Gate. Brother Aldobert led us in the Twenty-third Psalm.

"The Lord is my shepherd . . ." he began, and we all joined in, Judah ben Avram with as much reverence as the holy men.

Dame Joan turned on him with her most severe look.

"You have no business singing a holy Christian song," she said.

I wouldn't have chastised him, but his singing with us did seem odd.

"Most Esteemed Mistress," said Judah ben Avram. "I meant no offense. This is one of the beautiful songs of King David. I've been singing it all my life — mostly in Hebrew, but I know it in your tongue, as well."

Dame Joan seemed about to protest further. I don't think she fully understood what he was saying. King David was a Hebrew. We, in fact, were singing a Jewish song. I blushed for her, and my own ignorance.

"It is remarkable and very useful that our guide speaks our language so well," I said. "Isn't it, Dame Joan?"

"Yes, but . . ." She was not to be easily put off.

"And is it not splendid," Rhiannon joined in, "how the words of the great *Jewish* king have been preserved for us?"

Dame Joan was looking less peevish and more muddled. "I suppose," she said.

Simon looked over at me and winked.

"Let us all sing together," I said, linking Dame Joan's arm in mine.

We continued to sing. I sang and Dame Joan joined in, her voice tremulous and thin. Rhiannon, to my surprise, sang out loudly with jubilation.

And so we arrived at the Damascus Gate, our long journey ended, singing His praises.

XVI. Her Imperial Highness, Princess Edith

Our holy procession was soon overwhelmed in the crush of humans and animals pushing their way into the city. Were these souls seeking salvation, or simply trying to get the best spot at the marketplace? The guards at the gatehouse held up the caravan in front of us, demanding documents the caravan didn't seem to have. An argument broke out between the captain of the guard and the merchant with the most imposing turban. They spoke in what could have been a mixture of French and Arabic, making it impossible to follow what was going on. Soon the other guards and merchants joined in with shouts and laments. The camels complained and the donkeys brayed.

Behind us came another company of merchants and their beasts laden with goods, who claimed the right to bypass the first caravan. They pressed against us, shouting insults. The merchants in front of us and the guards responded in kind. Judah ben Avram started out calmly watching, but soon joined in the fray. It was impossible to tell what was really going on. Was this business as usual, or some special problem that would hold us up interminably?

Brother John tried to keep us singing. Only Brother Aldobert seemed able to concentrate. Brother Eustace, Simon, and Peter mumbled along a few words, before giving themselves up to the spectacle around us.

"Mother of God!" cried Dame Joan, falling into my arms as a camel blared right behind her.

Rhiannon and I tried to shelter her from the crush of men and animals. Dame Joan was chalk white and trembling so hard that in holding her I was trembling, too. I was very sorry we weren't still on our horses. At least then we'd be somewhat above this tumult instead of deep in it.

"Sir Raymond!" I called. "Judah ben Avram!" My burly knight pushed through to my side. Judah ben Avram left off arguing to join him.

"Dame Joan must be gotten out of this mess," I said. "Right now!"

Sir Raymond nodded, then spoke to Dame Joan. "By your leave."

Her response was a round-eyed look of terror. Sir Raymond scooped her up into his arms as easily as if she were a small child. He had the men form an arrow-shaped phalanx in front of them. The holy brothers, Rhiannon, and I flanked Sir Raymond. Peter and the servants brought up the rear with the horses.

"Honored Lady Edith," said Judah ben Avram, bowing. "Allow me to —"

"Do whatever you will," I said. "Just get us through this."

I thought he'd been shouting before. I was wrong. Judah ben Avram filled his lungs and bellowed. Words did not come out, only one long, deafening note that began low and ended high and shrill. It was louder than all the shouting men and bawling animals. All were stunned into silence. Then Judah ben Avram bellowed again.

"*Make way!*" he boomed. "Make way for Her Imperial Highness, Most Illustrious and Honorable, Princess Edith!"

Rhiannon grinned. "Your Highness," she said, and curtsied.

Lord, what trouble were we buying now?

"Princess Edith," said Sir Raymond, and smiled at me. "Well, why not? Forward!" he shouted. "March!"

The men pushed forward. The camels, donkeys, their drivers, the merchants, townspeople, and guards flattened themselves back against embankments and walls to let us through.

"Make way!" Judah ben Avram intoned. "Make way!"

Brothers John and Aldobert commenced to sing another hymn of thanksgiving. Brother Eustace was too dumbfounded and Simon was laughing too hard to join in. Dame Joan hid her face in Sir Raymond's shoulder. Rhiannon alone seemed comfortable with the situation. She proceeded forward perfectly composed. She was the one who might well pass as an imperial princess. She certainly could be the Welsh princess Tiborine had spoken of. Even if I'd had finer robes I didn't think I could impersonate the emperor's daughter.

This was unlike any entry into Jerusalem I could have possibly imagined. We'd started out a holy procession, become a carnival, and ended up marching in like the king's guard. I was grateful to Judah ben Avram for getting us past the merchants, but I didn't see how this pretense would get us through the Damascus Gate. Mightn't we all wind up imprisoned as impostors? I tried my best to imitate the hauteur of Rhiannon and marched forward.

Before we reached the gatehouse Judah ben Avram came to my side and spoke softly in my ear. "Honored Lady Edith, do not say a word, and I shall get us quickly into the city."

"With this deceit we might all quickly go to prison," I said.

"No, no. It will be all right," said Judah ben Avram. "I have a friend in the gatehouse. He will make everything go smoothly. Just pretend you don't understand . . ."

"That will be easy," I said. "For I don't understand any of it."

"Trust in God," he said and returned to the head of the company.

By the time we came to the gatehouse all the guards were formally lined up. As I approached they fell to one knee and saluted, all except the captain of the guard who eyed us suspiciously.

"Where is Her Imperial Highness's retinue?" he asked. "Where are her knights? Her baggage?"

"Her Imperial Highness wished to travel as a humble pilgrim," said Judah ben Avram.

I wondered if I should try to look humble, or maintain what I hoped was my imperial bearing. I glanced at Rhiannon, who stood erect and serene, and copied her.

"Furthermore, the Most Holy Roman Emperor, Conrad the Third, the princess's loving father, felt that she'd travel more safely incognito. And so he sent her first; her army of knights, servants, and baggage are coming soon after us."

"Where is the Imperial Seal?" demanded the captain.

"That and some secret documents from the Emperor are for Queen Melisende's eyes only."

"Hmph," he grunted. "Very well, my men will escort you to the queen. But I doubt you'll get round that she-devil."

It didn't appear that this was going as smoothly as Judah ben Avram had promised . . .

With one command the guards surrounded us, our horses, and baggage. As prisoners, we began our march through the streets of the Holy City.

"Judah ben Avram," I called, and he came to my side. "Is that surly captain your friend?" I whispered.

"No," said Judah ben Avram. "He is not my friend."

"Then shouldn't we call off this charade right now?"

"It will be all right," he said, but wasn't very convincing.

We were soon tramping through the warren of a marketplace, crowded with people, who stopped what they were doing to watch us pass. There were brown- and black-skinned people, veiled women, men with turbans or the little caps such as Judah ben Avram wore. There were also many Franks and Greeks, the women almost as heavily veiled as the Moslems. The streets smelled of all these people and the goods and produce that they sold. The scents of cardamom, ginger, oranges, cloves, and mint mingled with those of roasted lamb, wool, sweat, and offal. It was as if we were encased in a pomander. This Jerusalem was too earthly, too much of the senses, to be the Holy City.

"Were you expecting seraphs on street corners?" asked Rhiannon.

"Might not the houses at least shine with a heavenly light?" I said, and she smiled.

Curious comments followed us. The crowd seemed already informed about the imperial princess.

"I didn't know Conrad had another daughter," said one.

"Neither did I."

Dame Joan whimpered in Sir Raymond's arms. I hoped we could move the heart of Queen Melisende with her plight. Otherwise we might have journeyed all this way only to see the dungeons of the palace. Yet those around me didn't seem as concerned for our future as I. Were they pretending indifference to fool the guard? The holy brothers had returned to pious singing, except for Simon, who marched along with a glint of mischief in his eye. Rhiannon was also smiling. They both looked as if they were thoroughly enjoying this. Did they know of something that would extricate us from this predicament? Perhaps they trusted Judah ben Avram to lead us into a welcome as fine as that in the Bedouin's tent. I couldn't possibly keep up the pretense of being an imperial princess. Why couldn't Judah ben Avram have made me some insignificant little countess? Why not something I might possibly get away with? Sir Raymond looked calm. Yet hadn't he warned me about the queen? Why wasn't he worried?

Perhaps it was the heat. It was nearly all one could think about. The honey-colored stones soaked up the sun's rays and threw them back at us. It was an oven.

Was I the only one worried about this deception?

All the sense of hope I'd had short minutes ago upon entering the city, drained out of me. I couldn't breath. I could barely put one foot in front of the other. How could I face Queen Melisende, the "she-devil"? Oh, Lord! Help me!

XVII.
Queen Melisende

We were brought into a courtyard cooled by fountains and shaded by grape arbors and palm trees. Above us loomed the square tower that Judah ben Avram had pointed out to us from Montjoye — the Tower of David. Serenity and spaciousness replaced the press and noise of the streets. But the sun-baked smells of Jerusalem followed us into the Citadel. The very stones seemed mortared with cumin and clove.

Here we left the horses and all the servants except Peter. Judah ben Avram spoke a few words in Simon's ear, then Simon whispered something to Peter. Peter hastily unpacked a leather pouch before joining our procession through several other courts. The captain of the guard moved us briskly; I had only a fleeting impression of coolness and heavily scented flowers grown in huge pots. I had imagined that our first moments in Jerusalem would have been spent on our knees in the Church of the Holy Sepulcher in prayerful thanksgiving. Finding myself in the queen's palace was so unexpected that I felt as if I'd fallen into a dream.

We walked up twisting stairs and through cool, darkened rooms where men sat on cushions and ignored our passage. Eventually we came to a vast hall. Before reporting to the queen, the captain of the guard ordered the palace servants to see to our comfort. I wondered if all prisoners received such charitable treatment in the Holy Land, or if he was just being cautious in case I really was an imperial princess. Whatever the reason, I was grateful. Dame Joan was settled on a low bench against silken pillows. Servants appeared with basins of scented water to wash away the dust of our journey. I dabbed at her brow with a damp cloth and she began to regain her color and lose her look of terror.

Hot and cold drinks arrived, and tiny pies filled with fruit, nuts, and meat.

"First drink the hot," said Judah ben Avram. "It will quench your thirst."

I held the cup for Dame Joan as her hands still trembled, though mine weren't all that steady. "Better now?" I asked once the cup was drained.

"Yes." She sat up straighter and smoothed her skirts. "But what an inferno! That was clever of our guide getting us out of it."

"Now we have to confront the queen."

"I'd rather face twenty queens than suffer another camel," said Dame Joan.

I was glad she wasn't worried, and it was good to hear her sounding brave. Yet how many queens had my old nurse encountered? Didn't she realize that a queen might be a sight more formidable than a camel?

Was I the only one concerned for our precarious position? Sir Raymond, Peter, and the brothers were concentrating on the food and drink. Judah ben Avram sat by himself, lost in a reverie, or perhaps it was prayer. Rhiannon and Simon looked as if they were conspiring at something. I left Dame Joan and went to them.

"What shall I say to Queen Melisende?" I said.

"Say nothing," said Rhiannon. "But watch her carefully. I believe the queen has something to say to you."

"What is that supposed to mean?"

"Watch her and find out," said Rhiannon. "Meanwhile, let Judah ben Avram do all the talking."

"Trust your guide," said Simon. "I believe he has a plan."

"What?"

Simon shrugged, but there was that glint in his eye.

"Tell me," I said.

"I can't," he said. "Because I don't really know. Just wait and see."

"How can you be so calm?" I asked "At any moment we may find ourselves in the palace dungeon, instead of being pampered in the palace hall."

"We are in the city of miracles," said Rhiannon. "Can you not feel it?"

"No," I said, and went back to sit with Dame Joan.

Soon a page came to escort us to the royal chamber. We came into a room nearly as large as the hall, hung with silken tapestries. Courtiers were seated on benches around the room. They were dressed in pale, water-colored layers of tissue-thin silks, and engaged in various occupations that ceased upon our entry. The lutes, the books, the embroidery hoops were put to rest. All eyes were fixed on us, except those of the queen, who sat on a dais and continued to ply a golden needle with golden thread on scarlet silk. She was dressed all in diaphanous white embellished with fine gold filigree. Her skin was white as cream, but her brow and lashes were as dark as ebony.

We walked to the dais and stopped. Should I curtsy or remain standing? Dame Joan and Rhiannon dipped to the ground, then stood erect. I wasn't sure if an imperial princess would bow to a queen, but courtesy required something. I kept my head erect and bent my knees. Simon and the holy brothers bowed their heads, and Sir Raymond and Peter each fell to one knee. All was quite still; only the golden needle moved silently in and out of the silk. With each stab of the needle on the blood-red cloth I grew more and more anxious. Why didn't she look up at us? Wasn't she, at least, curious? What could I possibly learn from this aloof seamstress?

Judah ben Avram threw himself to the ground and wailed. "Oh, most noble, revered ruler of Jerusalem. Oh, Queen of the Holy City . . ."

"Remove him," said Queen Melisende, still without looking up.

Two guards materialized, lifted Judah ben Avram off the floor, and began to haul him away. The poor man seemed too shocked to speak. What did that mean, "Remove him"? Remove him from the room, or remove him forever? Something in the stillness of the courtiers convinced me that it was a death sentence. How could she? Surely his crime did not warrant death. Did she plan to execute us all? I looked around at Dame Joan, Rhiannon, and Simon. And they looked back at me, stunned. Clearly they didn't know what to do either. And they seemed as alarmed as I. Something had to be done.

"Stop!" I said, and knew it was terribly wrong the instant the word left my mouth. Some of the courtiers gasped. All seemed amazed. Yet, strangely enough, the guards halted halfway across the room.

Queen Melisende raised her dark eyes to meet mine. It was a chilling moment.

"Does her Imperial Highness speak?" she asked.

I wanted to squeak, "no," and scurry away to some dark hole. Instead I sank to the floor. My hands, looking for some support, found only the folds of my gown, to which I clung.

"Gracious Majesty," I faltered. It did come out much like a squeak.

If I was the frightened mouse, she was even more the cat. I saw it all in her cruel little smile. She could pounce at any moment, but first she'd play for a time with her prey. I couldn't bear that look of amusement. Well, I'd not give her the satisfaction of teasing the mouse. I stood up to face her, and caught Rhiannon's slight nod of approval as I did.

"There's been a mistake," I said, and this time I didn't squeak.

"Oh, and what might that be, Your Imperial Highness?"

"I am not an imperial princess. I am Lady Edith of Cheswick, from England."

The queen's lips curled. "Lady Edith of Cheswick?"

"Yes," I said. "Please liberate my guide."

She studied me for an interminable minute, then inclined her head ever so slightly. The guards let go of Judah ben Avram. From those around me came a faint, relieved sigh. Judah ben Avram moved smoothly across the floor and stood next to me.

The lords and ladies of the court remained in their frozen attitudes, still watching and waiting for their cat queen's next move.

Judah ben Avram spoke up. "My honored mistress has brought you a gift," he said, for once dispensing with flattery and flowery speech. He nodded to Simon, who took the leather pouch from Peter and stepped forward.

The queen inclined her head slightly, and an elderly lord quickly came forward to receive the leather pouch. He opened it and unwrapped the protective linen cloths, revealing sheaves of parchment. It was the psalter Simon had begun while we were in Rome. It had been commissioned by the pope, but Queen Melisende didn't need to know that.

As soon as she saw the psalter, the queen's face changed. Her eyes lost the look of the predator, or did they? Had she merely shifted the object of her pursuit? She beckoned the lord to bring the pages close to her. As he turned the leaves of Simon's beautiful illuminations the queen's cat smile became quite genuine.

"Whose work is this?" she asked.

"That of my brother, Simon, monk at Godstone Abbey," I said, and Simon bowed.

"It is exquisitely done," she said. "Lord Baldwin, have you ever seen such fine work?"

"Not in all the years I've lived, Your Majesty," he replied.

"So, the Lady Edith of Cheswick, who is *not* an imperial princess, has brought me a priceless gift."

The room remained still and tense. The cat queen wasn't finished toying with her prey. I tried to appear calm, and hold on to some shreds of my dignity.

"Welcome to Jerusalem, Lady Edith of Cheswick

and Simon of Godstone," said the queen, and her lips curled in what might have been a smile.

I felt the room relax. The courtiers now acknowledged us with cool smiles. The queen invited us to sit, and low benches were brought forward.

"Do tell me all about your travels," she said, and seemed truly interested in what Simon might say.

He managed her beautifully, just by being Simon. He told her of the scholars of Paris, and the glories of Rome. He wove into his tale a lifelong desire to visit Jerusalem, and meet Queen Melisende, renowned for her taste and appreciation of illuminated manuscripts. Simon appeared so guileless, even the cat queen seemed convinced. He told her the psalter wasn't yet complete because he'd waited to meet Her Majesty first, and discover her preferences for the book.

I was thankful that I needn't say anything. We all remained quite still, letting Simon weave his spell. There was no chastisement from Brother John about idle chatter, neither did Dame Joan venture an opinion. The cat queen was purring now, but I worried that at any second she might again show her claws. I watched her carefully, as Rhiannon had bidden me. But I couldn't imagine what counsel this frightening woman might have for me.

It was a long, worrisome audience. Eventually Queen Melisende was gently reminded by her chamberlain of another obligation, and we were dismissed.

"You have been a breath of fresh northern air," said the queen. "I hope that all you've told me of your travels will appear in my book."

"Whatever Your Majesty desires," said Simon.

"Don't leave out that fat cardinal," she said. And we were sent on our way.

"You could have let me know what you were going to do," I said once we got outside the palace to the hot street. I was trembling with anger and nerves.

"We didn't really know," said Simon.

Judah ben Avram was mopping his brow. "A thousand pardons, Honored Lady Edith," he said and bowed low before me. Then he turned to Simon. "And a thousand thanks to you, Revered Holy Brother. Your good deeds have saved me. I am forever in your debt."

Then he did something I'd never seen a man do with such abandon, — he cried. Tears ran down his face, and his body shook with wrenching sobs. I was too surprised to speak. We all just stood staring mutely at Judah ben Avram. It was Dame Joan who finally spoke.

"All's well that ends well," she said. She reached out and patted his shuddering back.

"But we might all have been killed by that she-devil." I, too, felt near tears.

Rhiannon took my hand. Her fingers were as cool as ever despite the suffocating heat. "It is over now," she said. "And we are all well."

"For now," I said. "What about later, what if the queen changes her mind?"

"Now she wants her psalter," said Simon.

"You mean, she wants the pope's psalter," I said.

Simon laughed.

"I think that we should give thanks," said Brother Eucstace.

"Yes," said Dame Joan, "as soon as we reach our lodgings."

"Judah ben Avram, do you have a plan for our accommodations?" asked Simon.

It was my duty to ask, but I was still too unnerved.

Judah ben Avram quickly stood, wiped his eyes, and loudly blew his nose on a square of silk. "I am your guide," he said. "I will take you to the best rooms in all of Jerusalem." He turned to me and bowed again. "With your permission, Honored Lady Edith."

Rhiannon gave me the slightest nudge.

"Yes, of course," I said.

Dame Joan, Rhiannon, and I mounted our horses. They looked as if they'd been well cared for during our interview with the cat queen. My little mare's coat was gleaming, and she didn't seem to mind carrying me again even after our arduous trek this morning. Yet I was nearly too tired to hold the reins. I hoped that the "best rooms in all of Jerusalem" were near at hand.

Once there, no matter how tired I was, I would kneel with the holy brothers and give thanks for our deliverance this day. Then I would pray for our continued safety because the city of the cat queen seemed a dangerous place. And I'd pray for myself.

XVIII. Revelations

I awoke to the sound of splashing water, and felt cool breezes. I slipped from my wide bed, careful not to disturb Dame Joan or Rhiannon, and tiptoed across the vast room to the window. Pulling aside the shade, I let in the dawn. Not far away, against the rosy sky, was the great golden dome of the Temple of the Lord, crowned with a golden cross. The muzziness of sleep left me instantly.

This was Jerusalem! It was my first morning in the city of the Savior. Not even the cat queen could alter that. Below my window was an enclosed garden. In the early light, I could make out palm trees and tubs of cascading flowers. Several fountains spilled into two large pools where amber and carnelian fish idled. Judah ben Avram had, indeed, found us the best rooms in all Jerusalem. In fact, the whole lovely house had been given over to us at his asking. Our cost was only the servants' wages, and our own supplies. Dame Joan couldn't believe it and kept trying to haggle with someone, although there was nothing to haggle over.

The air was delicious, cool and wonderfully fresh. Yet when I drew a breath there was still the oppressive weight on my chest that I'd carried all the long way from England. Perhaps I'd find a cure here. Perhaps not. I would try to be hopeful. As Rhiannon had said, this was the city of miracles.

I rested my head against the cool stones while the air set my curls to dancing. Since before my marriage, my hair had been kept carefully tucked into a wimple. I'd nearly forgotten the lovely feel of it loose and wild. Perhaps I could let it down more often. The thought blew around with my hair.

This breezy dawn was so different from the oppressive heat of yesterday. Maybe there were three cities here: the hot, fly-infested inferno, the temperate, lush city of dawn, and the realm of hope.

"It's the wind off the Mediterranean that makes it so cool," said Rhiannon at my side.

I put my arm around her thin shoulders and hugged her.

"I'm excited, too," she said.

I knew that. Rhiannon's thoughts now came to me almost as clearly as my own. It was time I knew her story.

Her blue eyes studied me, and she sighed. "Yes," she said. "It is time I told you. But it's a long tale, and a sad one, too."

"I'm listening."

"I don't like the telling."

"I know."

"My father was Griffith ap Rees, Prince of Cardigan. Gwenllian, daughter of the King of Gwynedd, was my mother."

I could hear the pride in her voice, just in saying their names. She was indeed a princess, and hadn't I always known that?

"My father, my grandfather, and my uncles fought the Norman invaders. When the Normans organized a great army against us, my father rode north to get help from my grandfather and uncles. Before he could return, the Normans struck. My mother put on armor and led our men against them. She died in battle, defending our home."

It wasn't hard to imagine Rhiannon's mother as a valorous knight. Rhiannon had that strength in her, as well.

"My father returned, and with the help of my grandfather and uncles, destroyed the Norman force. But, within the year, both my father and grandfather were dead. I was seven years of age."

"I'm so sorry," I said. Such inadequate words.

Rhiannon looked at me with all the little-girl sorrow writ plainly on her face. It had happened a long time ago. Yet I could see the pain was as new as yesterday.

"I was sent to France," she continued, "in the care of my father's sister, the Countess of Bordeaux."

"Just as Tiborine told me," I said.

She nodded.

"My aunt showed me every kindness. Last year she brought me back to Wales to celebrate the marriage of my brother, and to consider my own betrothal."

"And did you find a Welsh prince to suit you?"

"Nay. There were no thoughts of suitors for there was no wedding."

Rhiannon paused. Something terrible had happened in Wales. I waited for her to be able to speak it.

"My brother was murdered by my uncle."

"No!"

"Aye, awful, but true. In the chaos that followed, I was kidnapped by a Norman lord, and taken far away from the possibility of rescue, to a convent in Kent."

"That would explain your horror of the Good Sisters."

"You've no idea," said Rhiannon. "Worst of all, they planned to use me against my family. It could not be borne."

"So you escaped."

"Yes."

"And somehow you made it to the king's forest, where I found you."

"Where *I* found you." Rhiannon smiled.

"Thank you for finding me," I said. "But how did you manage it? How long were you in the king's forest? It must have been dreadful. Did you . . ."

Very gently Rhiannon put her hand over my mouth. Her eyes were filled with tears.

I nodded. She had told me enough for now.

"I shall keep you and your story safe," I said.

"I know," said Rhiannon and she kissed me. "Now, shall I tell you the story of Queen Melisende?"

"Must you?" I asked.

"Yes," she said.

I'd not protest. Rhiannon needed to leave behind the horror of her own story.

"Queen Melisende was married off to suit the needs of the kingdom, though she was in love with her young cousin," she said, beginning her tale.

This was uncomfortably familiar. Doubtless, it was meant to remind me of Will Belet. I didn't need to be reminded of him. But I wanted to keep my feelings for Will to myself, as Rhiannon surely knew.

"I don't want to hear any more," I said.

"All right," said Rhiannon. "I'll spare you the details. The point is that Melisende never had the chance to choose her fate and live her love. And you've seen what she's become."

"The cat queen," I said.

"Yes," said Rhiannon. "You have a chance. Don't wait for fate to choose you." Then she kissed me tenderly.

We stayed by the window watching the day begin. I thought of Will, and my quiet, secret love for him. Was he now in England? Did he think of me? I sighed.

Don't wait for fate to choose you. Rhiannon hadn't spoken, but I heard her words again.

The serenity of sunrise was soon swallowed up in the hurry and bustle of the day's start. Servants rushed about, fetching water, fuel, or fire. Merchants began to appear with enormous bundles of goods tied onto small sturdy donkeys. Shepherds drove flocks through the streets to pasture outside the city's walls. As the sun ascended the heat began to rise. The stone of the window ledge was no longer cool. The city of the inferno had begun its day.

"Princess Rhiannon," I said, curtsying before her. "Will your Grace honor me with your company on a tour of the Holy City?"

"Lady Edith," said Rhiannon. "As you already know, I will accompany you anywhere."

I kissed her hand, and we went to wake Dame Joan and dress.

"Let us go straightaway to the Church of the Holy Sepulcher," said Dame Joan, as we breakfasted on honeyed figs and flat bread in a hall open to the courtyard garden.

"Yes," said Brother Eustace. "It is our duty to go there first."

Brothers John and Aldobert nodded in agreement. Simon was too busy sketching the date palm in the garden to comment. But Judah ben Avram, who stood attendant at our table, looked very downcast.

"Ah, me," he sighed. "Such a pity, such a pity."

Rhiannon gave me a meaningful look.

"Perhaps our guide has other plans for us," I said.

"Honored Lady Edith, you are most perceptive," he said, now beaming.

"Tell us what you have in mind."

"I propose that this most holy and noble company follow in His footsteps, beginning with Christ's first introduction to Jerusalem when he was presented at the Temple. I will take you to all the holy places of His life, and that of the blessed Mother of God, before you travel the Via Dolorosa to the place of Christ's miracle — the Holy Sepulcher. Is it not a good plan?"

Dame Joan seemed doubtful, but Simon looked up from his drawing and smiled.

"It is an excellent plan," I said. "Let us go now before the sun gets any higher. Judah ben Avram, will you have the horses saddled?"

"We will leave the horses for now in their stable. They won't be needed until we go beyond the walls of the city to Mount Zion and the Garden of Gethsemane. But I have a surprise for the ladies. This way, please."

He led us to the gate of the house where six bearers were waiting with three canopied sedan chairs.

Dame Joan protested. "It isn't right to be carried. We are holy pilgrims, not idle Oriental ladies."

"Please, Gracious Ladies," said Judah ben Avram. "There is much walking from place to place, and many places to see. I don't want to tire you before you've begun."

Rhiannon and I might traipse all over the city, but I, too, saw the wisdom of sparing Dame Joan as much as possible.

"We'll walk later," I said. "Now we will follow the good advice of our guide." And I climbed into a chair.

"I don't like it," said Dame Joan, but she allowed Simon and Brother Eustace to help her into her chair. Rhiannon stepped lightly into hers. Judah ben Avram clapped his hands and two urchins appeared with drums. They marched at the head of our procession, banging heartily, and a path opened for us on the crowded street. So, we set out, as grand as pashas, to see the Temple of the Lord, where Jesus was presented as a boy.

"This is Mount Moriah," said Judah ben Avram, once we'd arrived on the high upper court of the Temple. Before us was the resplendent octagon crowned with a gleaming dome. Marbles of swirling patterns and colors sheathed the bottom half of the outer walls. The upper portions of the walls were covered with dazzling mosaics. It was a stunning sight, especially as the city all around us was dressed in sun-bleached colorless stones.

"On Mount Moriah," continued Judah ben Avram, "the history of the people of the One True God has its deepest roots."

"What are you speaking of?" asked Dame Joan.

"This most holy spot, Revered Mistress," said Judah ben Avram.

Dame Joan still looked puzzled.

"This was the temple of the Jews," said Rhiannon.

"What does that have to do with us?" said Dame Joan.

"Jesus was a Jew," said Simon.

"Oh."

Dame Joan looked chastened, and not very happy about it. I, also, felt reproved though I hadn't said anything. Although I knew perfectly well that Jesus was a Jew, it had never fully sunk in that He was a man such as Judah ben Avram. The Jews were so despised in England and all over Europe, yet Christ's family and the apostles were Jews.

"Are you all right, Lady Edith?" asked Judah ben Avram. "Perhaps the sun is already too strong?"

"No," I said. It wasn't the sun, but the shock of my vast ignorance. "Please continue."

"At the Lord's behest, Abraham brought his beloved only son, Isaac, to Mount Moriah. Abraham's love for the One True God was so strong that he was willing to sacrifice Isaac if that was what the Lord required."

"Do I know this story?" asked Dame Joan, looking confused.

"It is from the Bible, the Old Testament," said Brother Eustace.

"Oh," she said. "Did he kill Isaac?"

"No, the Angel of the Lord stay'd his hand," said Judah ben Avram. "The Lord God is merciful and just. He doesn't want the blood of children. The Jews have never practiced human sacrifice."

"But I've heard tales," said Dame Joan.

I'd heard those same tales, some told to me by Dame Joan, of Jews stealing Christian children to drink their blood.

"Those are only stories meant to frighten children," said Simon.

And to allow their elders to keep on hating Jews, I thought.

"Is it not sad, Lady Edith, the tales told by one people against another?" said Judah ben Avram.

I looked him in the eye. "It is shameful," I said.

He sighed. "Come into the coolness of the temple. I will tell you another story."

Inside, the walls and ceiling were covered with mosaics. Light streaming in the windows caught the bits of stone, and all the colors shone with unearthly splendor. We proceeded around the circuit of the choir in order to see it all. Above the arches supported by massive piers and delicate columns was a scroll with the text:

" 'My house shall be called the house of prayer,' says the Lord. 'In it whoever asks, receives, and whoever seeks, finds, and to anyone who knocks it shall be opened. Ask, and you shall receive; seek, and you shall find.'"

As often as I'd read those words, heard those words, and spoken them myself, they'd never had the weight, the intense meaning I found here in Jerusalem. For this was the house of the Lord. My heart was pounding.

The "Lord" of this temple wasn't Christ the Son of God. The cross on top of the dome misled me. This "Lord" was God, the Father, the father of Christ as well as Abraham, Isaac, and Jacob. It was an idea too big for me to contain.

Judah ben Avram drew Simon, Rhiannon, and me away from the others, and brought us to the center of the temple, where an expanse of rock was fenced round with fancy grillwork.

"This is the holy rock of Mount Moriah," he said, then lowered his voice to a whisper. "And here is something no Christian guide can tell you." He drew us into a close circle and looked furtively about.

"This building was not the Temple of the Jews," he said. "Before the Crusaders, it was a most holy shrine of the Saracens."

"No!" I said. "It cannot —"

Rhiannon shushed me with a look.

"When Mohammed went from Mecca on his winged horse in a magical night flight, he was transported to this place. See there, on the rock of Mount Moriah, is the hoofprint of his horse."

No. I couldn't believe this. For if I did, how could I believe the inscription above my head?

"You can believe both," said Rhiannon. "Be still and listen."

I would try, but it was difficult. Simon also looked uncomfortable.

"The greater truth," said Judah ben Avram, "is that Mohammed came to this rock because it is such a holy place. It is holy for the Jews and the Christians, too. Solomon's Temple, containing the Ark of the Covenant, was here. Jesus Christ was presented here as a little baby. This spot is sacred for us all."

I began to see. The holiness transcended history.

"When the Crusaders first came to liberate Jerusalem from the Saracens, many innocents were slaughtered here. The Crusaders were knee deep in the blood of women and children."

"*No!*" I didn't want to see that.

"Yes," he said and sighed. "Thousands of Jews and Moslems were murdered."

"It is unbearably sad," I said.

"What is, Lady Edith?" asked Dame Joan, coming over to us.

"Nothing," I said. At least Dame Joan couldn't read my mind. I didn't want her to see the bloody scene trapped in my head.

"I don't think being a guide is your true calling,"

said Simon to Judah ben Avram. "Being a rabbi better suits you."

"The Holy Brother esteems me far more than I deserve," said Judah ben Avram. "I am not a teacher; I am only a humble guide, wishing to show you the truth as I know it."

Judah ben Avram said the last to me and bowed.

I bowed in return. I'd come to Jerusalem, a pilgrim. I'd found more than I could, yet, understand. That didn't matter. I was in the right place, the Lord's Temple. It was time to ask and receive, to seek and find. It was time to open the door.

XIX.
In His Footsteps

From the Temple of the Lord we descended to the large open square at the foot of Mount Moriah.

"This is the Western Wall," said Judah ben Avram, indicating an expanse of ancient stone blocks. "This was one of the walls of the Holy of Holies. It is all that was left when the Romans destroyed the Temple."

There were a number of Jews standing in front of the wall, rocking as they prayed. Dame Joan, Rhiannon, and I left the sedan chairs to stand near enough to hear them. The odd sounding chanting was so different from our prayers.

"Yet I'm sure their intent is the same as ours," said Rhiannon.

"They pray for forgiveness, for the Lord's blessing, for peace," said Judah ben Avram, "and, most of all, for the Jews' return to Jerusalem."

The same and different.

We sang the holy office of Terce at the newly built

church of St. Anne. While we sang praises to the Lord, I thought of the Jews in the hot sun without their temple, in the city of David that they were not permitted to live in.

We were carried in the sedan chairs to the Zion Gate, where we were met by the servants with our horses.

"Now we will ride up the hill to see the Coenaculum, the Room of the Last Supper," said Judah ben Avram. "And if you wish it, the Tomb of King David."

"Yes," I said. "Let us honor the Hebrew king."

"Lady Edith!" said Dame Joan. "We cannot do that."

"Yes, we can," said Simon. "For Joseph was of the House of David."

"So he was," said Dame Joan, though she seemed doubtful.

"This is the only synagogue near Jerusalem that was not destroyed," said Judah ben Avram, as we entered the ancient building. Despite her misgivings, Dame Joan knelt with us and prayed in front of the tomb laden with symbols of the Jewish faith. What would have been anathema in England came easily here.

When we left the Tomb of David it was only a few steps farther along the narrow alley to the arched doorway of the Room of the Washing of the Feet. There we saw the marble basin where He had humbly knelt to cleanse the Apostles' feet. We climbed the steps leading to the Room of the Last Supper.

"Here Christ gathered the Apostles that they might celebrate the Passover together," said Judah ben Avram.

We were in a large airy room, of great simplicity. There were no paintings, no precious marbles, no tapestries. There was only the presence of the Lord.

"What is that pretty little apse?" asked Brother Eustace, once we had said our prayers. "And why is it empty?"

"It's a Moslem prayer niche," said Judah ben Avram. "It's called a Mihrab; it faces east in the direction of Mecca."

"Do you mean heathen Moors worshiped here?" Dame Joan asked.

Again I felt confused, too.

"The Moslems consider Jesus a great prophet," said Judah ben Avram. "Before the Crusaders, the Moslems came here to worship; it was a mosque."

"A mosque, here? That's impossible!" said Brother Aldobert.

"It is possible for believers in the One True God to worship at the same holy places," said Judah ben Avram. "I mean no offense, holy brothers, esteemed ladies, Sir Knight. I speak from the heart. Jews, Christians, Moslems, we are all of the same family."

No one said anything, though the holy brothers, Sir Raymond, and Dame Joan seemed to have difficulty accepting this. Nor was it easy for me to come round to thinking of the Saracens as my brothers, even though I could see the truth in it. Simon and Rhiannon looked as if they'd known this all along. How was that possible? It didn't seem like something Simon would have learned at Godstone. But my little brother had been much more in the world than I. His gift was in seeing the world with clear eyes. He and Rhiannon could see the truth of anything.

"Let us continue to follow in His footsteps to the Garden of Gethsemane," said Judah ben Avram.

Before we remounted, the servants poured us cool drinks. A donkey laden with baskets of food had come to join us.

"We will dine in the cool of a garden," said Judah ben Avram, "away from the hot stones of the city."

"You've provided for our comfort most thoughtfully," I said.

"Anything that I can do for you, Honored Lady Edith, will be done."

I was glad to get far enough away from the Holy City to distance myself some from its passions. Every stone in Jerusalem had been touched by either Christ, Mary, one of the Apostles, or by one of the ancient Jewish fathers. My head was swimming and my heart ached. There were so many stories, so many glorious yet sad endings. I began to suspect that Judah ben Avram really was a rabbi — a Jewish teacher. He was so intent on our seeing everything there was to be seen and hearing every tale ever told. He seemed to know the Christian stories as well as the holy brothers, if not better. So they listened respectfully to all his stories.

"Now we are crossing the Cedron Brook," said Judah ben Avram, "as Christ did when He came this way after the Last Supper."

"Then this is the valley of Jehoshaphat," said Brother John.

He must have lived in a Jerusalem in his mind for many years, for he always seemed to know where we were. I never did.

"Look back," said Judah ben Avram.

Directly behind and above us was the walled city.

"See the Golden Gate?" Judah ben Avram pointed to a bricked-up double gate in line with the Temple of the Lord. "The Jews believe that the southern gate, the Gate of Mercy, will open to the Messiah on the Day of Judgment."

"Our Messiah has already come," said Dame Joan.

"Yes, Esteemed Mistress," said Judah ben Avram quite humbly. "I know."

"There, there," she said, and patted his hand as she so often had patted mine, offering comfort to me in my sorrows or rages. "Yours will come soon enough."

My prickly old nurse was full of surprises.

We soon arrived at the Church of St. Mary. The church and convent were fortified with stout walls and a siege tower. They were reminders of the troubles that had been, and the still precarious state of the

Holy Land. Although believers in the "One True God" might worship the very same things, there were many among them intent on killing each other.

From the church porch, wide steps led us down out of the blinding sun to the cool, murky depths. Here was the crypt in which stood Mary's holy sepulcher. The air was thick with incense and smoking candles. Mosaics glittered all around the richly decorated crypt. On the ceiling was a painting of the Assumption. How tenderly Christ carried His mother, as if she were a little child. She who'd suffered so much in life, suffered nothing in death.

Hail Mary, full of grace, the Lord is with thee; blessed art thou among women. I thought of Mary in the grotto of Nazareth, met by the angel Gabriel. Once the angel explained her fate, she responded simply. "Here I am," she said, "handmaid of the Lord; as you have spoken, so be it."

How calm she was, far more than I. The day Dame Joan told me that I was not ill, but pregnant, I'd run away. I went as far into the woods as I dared, and wept cascades of angry tears. I felt trapped, terrified, and deeply ashamed of my fears. Only when evening came with a drenching rain did I return to Cheswick Manor, and the cosseting of Dame Joan. Oddly, she never scolded me for running away that day.

The next day I was less angry. The day after that, I was less fearful. Within a week I was so enamored of the child growing inside me, all my doubts took flight.

I looked over to where my old nurse knelt in prayer before Mary's tomb. She was glowing, as radiant as a maiden. All the fatigue and worry of our travels had been erased from her brow.

"Dame Joan is quite beautiful, isn't she?" said Rhiannon.

"Yes." Had she always been beautiful, and was I only now seeing it?

Simon appeared at my side.

"Look at Dame Joan," I said.

He nodded. "She looks younger than you, Edith."

She did, indeed.

"Judah ben Avram sent word that a meal awaits us in the garden if it suits you."

Rhiannon helped me collect Dame Joan, and Simon shepherded the holy brothers back up to the intense heat and glare of midday. Not far from the church was the walled grove of ancient olive trees, the Garden of Gethsemane. Many of the trees were held up by crutches, supporting decrepit limbs. There was such antiquity here; I felt it more palpably than in the ancient city. I'd never seen anything like these venerable living things. Most impressive of all was the tree to which Judah ben Avram led us. It was as big around as several sturdy knights. Part of the trunk was split open and hollow. All was gnarled and bent in upon itself, yet the twisted limbs still bore fruit.

"This great-great-great-grandfather was bearing fruit when Jesus came here at the hour of His betrayal," said Judah ben Avram. "When no man would offer comfort to the Son of God, this sacred tree stood by as His witness."

"This very tree was with Christ?" asked Sir Raymond. He looked more awestruck than at any other moment of our journey.

"This tree, yes," said Judah ben Avram.

Sir Raymond knelt before the contortion of limbs and trunk. "This tree has seen the living Christ?"

The more Sir Raymond marveled, the more I appreciated this miracle of age. Leaving the city walls didn't remove us from the passions of the past. The earth was permeated with what had been. Christ's moment of abandonment and despair was to be read in the tree before me.

"Nearby are shade and the cool water of a fountain," said Judah ben Avram. "Let us rest and eat."

We followed him down a path to a shaded veranda, where the air was cooler. Basins of water were readied for our ablutions. The repast was laid out on white linen, and looked delicious.

When I was settled on a cool stone bench, Judah ben Avram handed me a sprig off a flowering bush. "Hyssop," he said.

The small white flowers were delicately scented.

"'Purge me with hyssop, and I shall be clean . . .'" said Simon.

"What psalm is that?" asked Dame Joan.

"The fifty-first," said Brother Aldobert. "'. . . Wash me and I shall be whiter than snow.'"

That is what I wanted: to be emptied clean of the worries that pursued me.

Rhiannon waited until the others were in a heated debate over which psalm was the most beautiful before asking, "What worries?"

"Sir Runcival," I said. "Pope Lucius, and the good Queen Melisende."

"Those are not your real worries," she said.

They seemed real enough to me.

"You have yet to name your real worries and sorrows," said Rhiannon. "But that you must come to on your own."

"Don't you think I ought to be worried about Queen Melisende?" I asked.

Rhiannon's brow wrinkled momentarily. "No," she said. "You might worry about becoming like her, but she is so pleased with Brother Simon's psalter, why should she harm any of us?"

"That may be, but she is still dangerous," I said.

"Only if you put yourself in her way. And you won't do that again, will you?"

I'd do all that I could to avoid the cat queen.

"What about Pope Lucius?" I said. "Shouldn't I be concerned about his plans for me? You were troubled by them when we were in Rome."

"When we were in Rome we were subject to the

pope's rule, and dangerously close to St. Cecilia's. The pontiff is really interested only in Simon's art. He'll find other ways to entice Simon. And I don't think your brother would mind spending a few years in the Holy City, do you?"

Simon would be happy in Rome. As long as he could work, he would be happy nearly anywhere, even without me.

"Now consider Sir Runcival," said Rhiannon.

"I'd rather not."

"Do you think he still pursues you?"

I saw the merry look in her eyes and knew the answer.

"Perhaps not." If he had pursued me, surely he'd have caught up with me by now. "But won't he still be waiting for me?"

"Do you think you are the only wealthy widow in England?" she asked. "As charming as you are, Lady Edith, Sir Runcival won't have waited for you this long."

"There could well be another Sir Runcival," I said. "There are more impoverished knights than there are wealthy widows to go around."

"So, command your fate," she said. "Choose your own knight."

Choose or be chosen, she was right. Choosing was better.

XX.
Peregrine

The sun was setting as Judah ben Avram brought us to the door of the Church of the Holy Sepulcher.

"Honorable Lady Edith," he said. "I will return within the hour to escort you to your lodgings." He bowed and departed with the yeomen leading all the horses.

We entered the great hall of the church, called the Katholican. Each of us sank to the ground in deep obeisance before the ornate choir screen.

"Let us pray," said Brother John.

"We give thanks, Oh merciful Father, for our safe deliverance," said Brother Aldobert. His voice trembled with emotion.

Brother Eustace continued, "Our Father who art in heaven, hallowed be thy name . . ."

Everyone joined in except me. My lips ought to have spoken the prayer with the others. My heart should have been filled with gratitude for coming safely all this way. My thoughts ought to have been only upon the Lord and His infinite wisdom and mercy. But I was too distracted to devote my heart to the Lord. Rhiannon had dismissed my worries as groundless. She said I had yet to name my real worries and sorrows. What were they? What kept me from drawing a breath without choking? What was haunting me if not Sir Runcival, if not Pope Lucius, if not Queen Melisende?

In Jerusalem, I'd come to the end of my peregrination. I had to think about what I would do with the rest of my life. I couldn't spend it running away from phantoms, nor in perpetual pilgrimage. I had to settle on a life and live it. But what life? All I knew was what I didn't want. I didn't want to wed Sir Runcival. I didn't want to be shut up in St. Cecilia's. I particularly did not want to end up like the heartless queen. What did I want? Choose or be chosen.

I felt a sharp twinge. Rhiannon, whose hands were clasped in prayer, hadn't pinched me, though she certainly looked capable of it. I heard her thoughts as clearly as if she spoke them: "You have traveled a great distance to be here. You must put your concerns aside for now."

"Thy kingdom come, thy will be done."

She was right. My thoughts were keeping me from this sacred spot, the goal of my pilgrimage. I began to look around me as the holy brothers continued their prayers. Above the high altar was a painting of the Virgin holding the Christ Child. I had held my babe as tightly as Mary held hers, as if I could have shielded her. I couldn't, any more than Mary could have kept her child from His fate.

Cistercian monks in purest white and Greek fathers in austere black came through separate doors, carrying honeyed candles and censers. Heavily perfumed smoke wafted around their robes, and clouded the hall. The service for Vespers was about to begin. One young Cistercian began the holy office, singing high and clear. Deeper voices rose to meet his from across the hall. Brothers John, Aldobert, Eustace, and Simon joined in. Soon all the monks were singing His praises in harmonious plainsong.

I tried to remember back to when I had first left Cheswick Manor to journey here. Then, I'd never been beyond Oxfordshire or Surrey; now, I was in Jerusalem. The litany of place names sang inside my head: *Godstone, Dover, Boulogne* . . . It was hard to comprehend all that I'd seen and done since leaving England . . . *St. Denis, Paris, Vezelay, Lyons, Sarenom* . . .

I'd once told Will Belet that I longed to be a crusading knight and travel to the Outremer. He suggested that I might go as a pilgrim. Perhaps that is when this journey began — when Will planted the seed of it so long ago. It was before my betrothal and marriage. It was before my babe was born, and before she died. When I still believed my life could be an adventure. I'd left England to leave behind my life, and to escape from marriage to Sir Runcival. But, day by day, and week by week, this journey had become a true pilgrimage. I'd crossed lands and seas and come to the Outremer. Had I arrived any closer to His divine grace? I tried to listen to the plainsong for anything that He might say.

Dame Joan was singing beside me. Her face was bathed in tears, yet beautiful. Rhiannon, too, was singing. Rhiannon, who never seemed comfortable in a church, and who never before had spoken a word of Latin, was effortlessly singing. Even Sir Raymond sang the responses. Only Peter and I were mute among our company. I'd have to take a greater hand in Peter's education. My page shouldn't be so ignorant. But why wasn't I singing with the others?

. . . *Marseille, Rome, Bari* . . .

The incense and song washed over me like the waves of the sea. A few paces to my right was the Omphalus, the sacred center of the world. Surely here I could find my place in the Lord's plan. The Holy office continued, yet I was unable to hear the words, only the pounding of my heart. *Dalmatia, Greece, Constantinople* . . .

We weren't the only pilgrims. Many others knelt and sang His praises. There were old people and young, men and women. They'd left their homes to walk in Christ's footsteps, to know His suffering, and to earn His grace. Some women sobbed. Some men did, too. There was such strong feeling around me. I was in it, yet not a part of it.

Vespers ended. Rhiannon, Peter, and I helped Dame Joan to her feet. We followed Simon and the brothers in procession behind the choir to the rotunda. In its center was the chapel built over the Holy Sepulcher. The dome above us, as vast as heaven, rested on huge stone piers. Between the heaven of the dome and the columns was a wide band of glowing mosaics. There was Jesus as a sweet-faced boy. On His left hand was his mother; on His right was the archangel Gabriel proclaiming, "Hail Mary, full of grace; the Lord is with thee, blessed art thou amongst women, and blessed is the fruit of thy womb."

While Jesus lived she had been blessed.

We walked the full circle of the rotunda to come to the northern entry of the tiny chapel. Here we waited. The chapel of the Holy Sepulcher could admit only a few people at a time, and a number of people were ahead of us. I listened to the cries of those who preceded us.

"Oh blessed Lord!"

"Redeemer!"

"Savior!"

Such wrenching cries, the walls rang with their zeal.

The pilgrims seemed to experience Christ's passion as their own. My soul reflected the heat of their fervor.

When it was our turn, a Greek priest ushered us into the chapel. Inside, another priest gave us candles. Sparkling all around us in the flickering light were mosaics showing the scene of Christ's burial. My heart began to race.

"Oh my Redeemer!"

"Blessed Savior!"

I couldn't breathe. Before me was the face of Mary, riven with sorrow. Once she had been a hopeful, if anxious, mother, as I had been. Now her grief seemed unbearable. I knew that grieving. I'd felt my child's heart stop beating, and my own cleave in two.

In Mary's infinite sorrow I found my own. My child was dead and my arms were empty.

"Precious Lord!"

"Christ!"

"This way," said the priest. We crawled on hands and knees through the low mouth of the sepulcher. Simon and Peter went first and helped pull Dame Joan and me through the opening. All the while, a keening sorrow was pushing up from my stomach, to my chest, the sadness that I'd thought was safely locked within me. I tried to hold it in my throat, and clung to Dame Joan.

We entered a cramped chamber where hundreds of candles burned. We lit our candles and set them on the altar. The chamber was thick with smoke and incense, and terribly hot. White marble, gold, and precious stones covered the sepulcher. Along the sides were three holes. Through them Dame Joan and the holy brothers kissed the very stone where Christ had lain. I could not do that. I could not . . .

When I saw the sacred stone, I did not think of the man, but of the Christ child — and my own child buried in the cold earth. The sorrow in my throat would be held no longer. It broke from me in a loud, low wail.

"NO!" I cried, unable to contain it. The walls of the sepulcher echoed my pain. I covered my mouth with both hands. "NOOOOOO!" I could not stop myself. I fell to the ground, and still I cried. I howled. I sobbed. I saw the stricken look on Dame Joan's face, and on Peter's and Simon's. Yet I could not stop. Rhiannon petted me, and said words that I could not hear for my own mad screaming.

Lord, what was happening to me?

Rhiannon and Simon tried to hold me, but I fought them like a wild thing. Breaking free, I clawed my way out of the tomb, and out of the chapel. The rotunda was a blur of pilgrims. I got to my feet, but sobs shook my body. I was just barely able to keep the howling inside my head. I had to find a place to hide.

Across from where I stood was a large somber chapel. I staggered into it. One lone monk prayed at its altar. I took myself away from him to the darkest corner. An opening in the wall revealed dimly lit, rough-hewn stone steps. I followed them down to a stark cave cut from the living rock. In it was a small, plain altar where several candles flickered. I was alone. I sat on a bench carved out of the wall, and let myself cry out all the sadness I'd held back. Over and over, I relived the moment when my child died. I raged. I wept. Grieving without end. And yet, in time, the sorrow and the anger began to ebb. I let the cold stone soothe me. Gradually my sobs ceased. I took a deep shuddering breath, mopped up my tears, and blew my nose.

I was a sodden mess. I pulled off my wimple and outer robe, and shook out my hair. No one would disturb me in this lonely spot. Rhiannon would have held back Dame Joan and Simon. She'd know that I needed time by myself. I listened a moment for footsteps, and heard the silence of eternity. On the wall by the altar was scratched, "Joseph of Arimathea." He had given his sepulcher that Christ might be decently buried. I knelt before his altar.

"Thank you for shelter," I whispered. Then I stretched out, full-length, on the stone flags.

How cold and comfortable it was. I closed my eyes. I breathed deeply. In and out, my breath came so easily. I lay still, simply breathing. Gone was the grief that had choked me for so long. Emptied of the mad, animal wailing, I felt peace. Empty of anguish, filled with peace. Each new breath released sorrow, and let in His light. I'd found His grace.

Gentle sadness returned and I wept easy tears for the joy I'd had and lost, and grateful tears for what I'd found.

I could hear Rhiannon speaking in my mind, "You've clung to her with your sorrow. Now will you finally let her go?"

"I'll try," I said.

"Trying is not enough."

I opened my eyes. Rhiannon was leaning over me, the curtain of her hair shrouding her face.

"What else can I do, but try?"

"In all the time we've been together, you've never once named your child."

"She had a name," I said.

"But you never even think it."

"No."

"Give her her name, and let her fly away," said Rhiannon. "She is the peregrine who must be allowed to go."

"She is too little to go alone."

"She is not alone, but in God's hand. Let Him take care of her."

She was in God's hand. But I wanted to keep her still with me. I closed my eyes again, and looked for the face of my little one. I saw her dimly, veiled by the time already passed. I tried holding my breath to see if that would make her face clear to me. No. She was already on her own journey. I could not — I would not — hold her back.

"Alice," I said. "Her name was Alice." And I let my child go.

XXI.
Empty and Full

By the time Rhiannon and I emerged from the smoky gloom of the Holy Sepulcher, night had fallen. Cool winds blew through the streets. The pestering flies were, at last, defeated. The hot-spice smells of cardamom, clove, and cumin that ruled the day were dissipating in the breeze. Now the scents of jasmine, rosemary, and myrtle infused the streets. It was glorious to inhale Jerusalem at night. I was drained of sorrow, filled with light. Empty and full, my life was ready to begin anew.

Simon and Judah ben Avram were waiting with two sedan chairs and their bearers.

Simon came to me, took my hand and looked into my eyes.

"You've found what you've been looking for," he said.

I nodded.

Simon kissed my brow. "Bless you, Edith."

"Thank you, Simon."

"Honored Lady Edith," said Judah ben Avram. "May I escort you to your lodgings?"

"Please, but I would walk if you don't mind."

"That suits me, as well," said Rhiannon. "Perhaps Brother Simon will ride. He's been walking all day."

"You forget my calling, Mistress Rhiannon," said Simon. "A sedan chair is not seemly for a monk. Besides Brothers John or Aldobert would be sure to catch me. Then there would be Hell to pay."

"May you never have Hell to pay," I said.

Simon's face grew serious. "In this life we cannot elude our troubles. They will always catch up with us."

"Have you always seen so clearly into the heart of things?" I asked.

"Your heart I have clearly seen. Now that I see it unfettered, I am glad for you."

"Let's go to Dame Joan," said Rhiannon. "She needs to know that all is well with you."

"If I may speak," said Judah ben Avram.

How unusual for him to ask permission.

"Yes, of course, Sage and Cherished Guide."

He smiled.

"When I accompanied the Esteemed Mistress to your lodgings she was most joyful. She sang the praises of the Lord on high for releasing Honored Lady Edith from her sorrow."

Was I so transparent? Did they all know me so much better than I knew myself?

Rhiannon smiled at me.

"It's always much easier to read another's story than to understand one's own," she said.

"But I've only seen a small part of your story," I said.

"Is that so?" She looked at me with teasing eyes.

"Perhaps I know enough for now," I said. " I know you were sent to help me find my own story. The rest will come."

"Aye," said Rhiannon. "You will see, I am clear as glass."

Judah ben Avram led the way through the darkened streets. The two urchins, who'd banged the drums this morning, now carried torches to light our way. I was so tired, yet so wide awake. Everything around me seemed distinct. As dark as it was, nothing was murky. For once my path was clear. I walked between Rhiannon and Simon, my fingers laced in theirs.

"So, tell me how my story will end?" I asked Rhiannon.

"You know that," she said.

Yes, I did. It would end with Will Belet. But what if Will had changed in ways I could not know? What if he was no longer the man that I had loved?

"Is that possible?" asked Rhiannon.

I thought back to when I met Will Belet. We were both children then. From the first moment I'd seen him, I knew that he loved me, and I loved him. When last I'd seen him, he'd become a man. He'd been through trials of the kind that could harden a heart and coarsen a soul. Yet Will had always been true and good. Nothing would change that. Nothing would change him.

But what if I had changed too much for Will to still love me? I was not the girl I had been.

"If Will Belet is a grown man, why would he want to share his life with a girl?" said Rhiannon.

"You're right," I said.

"Then it's settled," said Rhiannon.

"What is settled?" asked Simon.

"Lady Edith's future," said Rhiannon.

"I will return to England," I said.

"Yes, and?" said Simon.

"And I will find Will Belet."

"That is a plan that suits you," said Simon.

"And it will make a good tale," said Rhiannon, "the story of your going and your going back, complete with happy ending."

"I cannot write the ending yet," I said, "not before I've lived it."

"No," said Rhiannon, "not quite yet."

"And you, Simon," I said. "What will your story be?"

"I will finish the pope's psalter for the queen," he said. "Then I'll begin another for the pontiff. His will have many scenes of the Holy Land and Constantinople. Mistress Rhiannon, what is your plan?"

She smiled. For once, I didn't need to ask. I already knew. Rhiannon would stay with me until she was ready to choose her own knight.

"You will not return to your family?" asked Simon.

"There is no one left to go back to," she said.

I was her family.

"Thank you for choosing me," I said.

"I chose well," she said.

This was how my journey would end and begin.

All the life I'd lived had brought me to this point. I couldn't change what had been, nor would I want to. I'd known great joy in the birth of my daughter, Alice. I'd had the gift of a kind husband. His generosity had allowed me more scope than most women ever dreamed of.

I was the peregrine, flying freely all the way to the Holy Land and back to roost in England. England was where I was meant to be; I knew that now. I felt it in my bones. I could return to a home of my own. I need not stay as an unwanted guest at Cheswick. I didn't have to consign myself to Woburn Abbey. Neither did I have to live under my father's roof. I could be as bold as the namesake of Rhiannon, the Welsh princess she'd told me about so long ago. I could seek out Will Belet. It wouldn't be hard to find him. He would be at the court of young Prince Henry. I could walk right up to him and say:

"Will Belet, you are the only man I'll have in marriage, and I've come to hear your answer."

My heart raced at that thought. But I knew I could say it because it was true. Will was my dearest friend, my love. I could tell him that because now I was free.

THE END

Author's Note

While researching *Peregrine* I discovered some of the wonderful women that Edith encountered on her journey: Bertrade de Montfort; Rhiannon, daughter of Heveydd Hen, from the Welsh saga, The Mabinoqion; the women poets, the *trobairitz* of Provence — including the three Tibors; Queen Melisende of Jerusalem; Gwenllian of Wales; and Dame Margery Kempe. I was already familiar with the tragic Heloise and the dynamic Eleanor of Aquitaine. Remarkably, nearly all of these women were contemporaries of Edith, my twelfth-century heroine. The one exception was Dame Margery. But I was too fond of this eccentric pilgrim to exclude her from my story just because she lived some hundred and fifty years after the events of *Peregrine*.

I began writing *Peregrine* because I was worried about Edith at the end of my book, *The Winter Hare*. She had such spirit; I didn't want her trapped in a life without love or adventure. Edith had dreamed of traveling to the Holy Land. I wanted to make that dream come true. But Edith had to pay a terrible price for that to happen.

A medieval girl belonged to her father. Once wed, a woman and all her property belonged to her husband. Only in widowhood could a medieval woman control her property and her fate. Only as a widow could Edith embark on a journey of her own.

I'd traveled in England, France, and Italy, but I'd never been to Israel. I read books about Jerusalem. I even found *A Guide to the Holy Land*, written by Theoderich, the monk, in 1173! Yet as much as I could read and study about Jerusalem, I felt I had to experience the city in order to write about it. So I left my family and journeyed to the Holy Land. It was a thrilling and deeply moving experience. And I am extremely grateful to Edith for inspiring my own pilgrimage.